'What were you escaping from?'

Cam swallowed the last mouthful of his food and pushed the plate away. He topped up his tea and said slowly, 'Andie, there's no need to make my being here the reason for chucking in this job before you've even started. Just treat it as an unfortunate coincidence.'

'Don't you think it will make working together difficult?'

'Why should it? It wasn't me you married.'

Dear Reader

Can you put the past behind you? Jenny Ashe poses this question in THE CALL OF LOVE, while Sarah Franklin looks at obsessive behaviour in THE WESSEX SUMMER. No claims for a cure, but sometimes help can be found. In WAITING GAME, Laura MacDonald explores the passage from infatuation to love, in a touching story, while Judith Worthy gives us a heroine who married the wrong brother—the right one is *very* right. . . Australian Cam Walters is every woman's dream!

See you next month!

The Editor

Judith Worthy lives in an outer suburb of Melbourne, Australia, with her husband. When not writing, she can usually be found bird-watching or gardening. She also likes to listen to music, and the radio, paints a little, likes to travel, and is concerned about conservation and animal cruelty. As well as romantic fiction, she also writes books for children.

Recent titles by the same author:

CROSSROADS OF THE HEART
DEADLINE LOVE

A HEART UNTAMED

BY

JUDITH WORTHY

MILLS & BOON LIMITED
ETON HOUSE   18–24 PARADISE ROAD
RICHMOND   SURREY   TW9 1SR

First published in Great Britain 1992 by Mills & Boon Limited

© Judith Worthy 1992

Australian copyright 1992 Philippine copyright 1992 This edition 1992

ISBN 0 263 77779 0

Set in 10 on 10½ pt Linotron Times 03-9207-58923

Typeset in Great Britain by Centracet, Cambridge Made and printed in Great Britain

CHAPTER ONE

'PHEW! Thank goodness. . .'

Relieved to have arrived at last, Andie parked her car alongside two others in the one patch of shade in the hospital car park, under an enormous gum tree. As the dust subsided, she got out and glanced up into its gnarled branches. A drowsy kookaburra on a low branch cocked an eye at her, then closed it. It was too hot to laugh at her.

Andie was laughing a lot at herself, though. Somewhat ruefully. She must have been mad to come here, right to the edge of civilisation, but at least she wasn't likely to bump into Paul, and since he would have no idea where she'd gone he wouldn't be telephoning. Andie sighed. There had been a time when she had thrilled to his voice at the end of a telephone line, especially when she'd been in London and he had been in Sydney.

'Well, I'd better go in and let them know I'm here.' She slung her handbag over her shoulder, but left her luggage until she knew where she would be staying.

Everything had been rather vague, but the agency had assured her that there would be 'no problems'. She'd taken that with a grain of salt, and perhaps she should have demanded a few more details, but she'd been so anxious to get away that she had accepted the job come what may.

She was locking the car door when a horn tooted impatiently—no, imperiously, behind her. Andie glanced over her shoulder. A Range Rover was almost ramming her back bumper, looming over her modest hatchback like a tank. Reflections made it impossible to see the driver, but she felt instant antagonism for

5

the unseen horn blaster. She'd got the message—she
had parked in someone else's spot—but there was no
need for rudeness.

A head jerked out of the Range Rover's driving
window. Male. Naturally. He was wearing a slouch hat
and Polaroids. Outback macho man, she thought
derisively.

'The visitors' car park's over there,' a brusque voice
told her. He jerked his thumb over his shoulder.

The head disappeared, leaving Andie with the curious feeling that she'd met him before somewhere.
Hadn't a voice like that sent shivers down her spine
. . .shivers of anger. . .?

'Keep your hair on, I'll move,' she muttered, drop-
ping back into the driving seat. Her fingers beating a
tattoo on the steering wheel, she glanced in the rear-
view mirror. She couldn't move until he did. He
moved, but not the vehicle. He slid out, a long lean
man with broad shoulders, slim hips and a way of
walking that combined arrogance with the languid
grace of a feline animal—of the big cat species. His
khaki shirt was unbuttoned to the waist, showing a
sprinkling of dark hair on an olive-skinned muscular
chest, a sinewy throat and neck. His shirtsleeves were
rolled up to his elbows and clung to taut biceps, while
his jeans fitted smoothly over prominent calf and thigh
muscles. A well-built man, rugged, hewn by the out-
doors. . . Andie's assessment abruptly ended as he
came nearer and her gaze fixed on his face. She drew
in a sharp breath.

No, no, it *couldn't* be. . . She stared, dry-mouthed
all at once, heart pounding. *He* couldn't be *here*. It
was impossible. She was hallucinating; this man just
looked a little like him. He passed out of range of her
rear-view mirror, and a moment later his face appeared
at the driving window. He pushed his sunglasses up on
to his forehead and stared at her.

'It's OK,' he said in a more amenable tone. 'You

might as well stay here now.' The smile was presumably to take the edge off his former brusqueness. Without the distortion of the mirror he looked less formidable.

Andie could feel beads of perspiration forming on her upper lip, and her knees were trembling. There was no mistaking those dark, censorious eyes. It *was* him! But he hadn't recognised her yet. The headscarf covering her pinned-up long blonde hair, the large wrap-around dark glasses she was wearing, were adequate disguise. After all, he hadn't seen her for five years, and back then only a few times. And today, here, she would be the last person he'd expect to see.

Andie's instinct was to get the hell out of there as fast as possible before he recognised her, but his Range Rover was blocking her exit. Another car hemmed her in on one side, a fence on the other. She couldn't move unless he did.

'Thanks.' She lowered her tone a little, mustered a faint smile. 'Sorry.' If she said too much, he might recognise her voice.

He was staring at her, but there was no recognition in his eyes yet. Perhaps he was a mirage, like the ones she'd seen ahead of her almost all the way from Adelaide, that would prove to have no substance. But something as solid as that big masculine frame wasn't about to evaporate.

'I'll shift back a bit so you can get out later,' he said. He jerked his thumb up at the tree. 'We're a bit selfish about the shade.'

'*I'll* move. . .' she began.

'No, please. . .it's OK.'

His tone was warm, mellow, almost kindly. It was not a tone she had ever heard from him. She shivered again as she thought of the scathing tirade she had had to endure five years ago. But she'd won, and he had never forgiven her for that, she knew. Dr Cameron

Walters was not a man to take defeat lightly. The galling part was that her victory had been hollow.

He moved his vehicle back slightly to give her room to manoeuvre, then leapt out and strode towards the hospital entrance. Shaken, Andie watched. The last time she had seen him, all that muscular physique had been hiding under an expensively tailored grey suit, crisp white shirt and maroon tie with gold tiepin. She remembered every detail vividly, every word that had been spoken.

I'm going, she decided. I'm not staying here—I *can't*. I can't work with *him*. She had no doubt that Dr Cameron Walters worked at the Boobera Hospital. Even if he was just one of the local visiting medicos, it would still be impossible. He wouldn't want her there anyway.

Andie wiped a hand across her brow. It came away damp and grimy. She was hot and tired and suddenly tearful. What a way for it to end! The Great Escape! Great *Disaster*! Crashing its gears, she turned the car towards the entrance. No doubt Cam would eventually discover that the woman who had briefly occupied his car space was Andrea Somers, his brother's ex-wife, who had taken a job at the hospital and then run off without even going in. She wondered grimly if he would let on that he knew her. Probably not. Cam had long since ceased to acknowledge her existence.

As she swung the wheels around, the engine suddenly coughed and died. Andie remonstrated with it impatiently and turned the key. When nothing happened her eye fell on the fuel gauge. Empty. She must have only just made it to the hospital. Chagrined, she beat her fists on the steering-wheel. What now? It was Sunday and on her way through she had noticed that what seemed to be the town's only petrol station had been closed like everything else. She could walk there and hope to knock someone up, but the more sensible course was to go into the hospital first and find out if that was how to get petrol on a Sunday. That would mean telling them she'd decided not to take the job after all, which in all conscience she ought to do anyway.

You can't just cut and run, she told herself, appalled that she should have even considered it. That wouldn't be fair. But what would she tell them? That she hadn't expected it would be so remote. . .so hot. . . Would they believe that? There was nothing she could think of that didn't sound lame. What a prize ninny they would think her.

Wearily, Andie got out of the car and again locked the driver's door. She threw the four-wheel-drive a baleful look and walked up to the hospital entrance. What in heaven's name was Cam doing here? Five years ago he had been a senior registrar in a big Sydney hospital. Paul hadn't said anything—but of course until recently she hadn't seen Paul for three years, and lately he hadn't been telephoning her to tell her about his brother.

It was refreshingly cool inside the white-painted wooden building and the hum of air-conditioning was a low background noise in what was otherwise a stillness that made Andie instinctively think 'crisis'. There seemed to be no one on duty at the reception desk, so she sat down on a plastic chair in a nearby waiting area and idly leafed through an old, very dog-eared *National Geographic*.

It was five minutes before anyone appeared, and then a somewhat harassed-looking woman in a blue nurse's uniform came at speed along the corridor, stopped momentarily at the sight of Andie, then came across to her, smiling.

'Andrea Somers?'

'Yes. . .I. . .'

'Sorry, I'm afraid I forgot all about you. It's been panic stations here today.' The nurse smoothed straight red hair back behind her ears and smiled a

real welcome. She clasped Andie's hand warmly. 'Am
I glad to see you!' She rushed on, 'But I'm afraid I
can't stop. There's a bad RTA coming in—a head-on
collision out on the Tuttumburra Road, two cars, one
trailing a caravan. God knows what state they'll be in,
poor devils. It's a two-hour drive each way at the best
of times——' She broke off as the wailing of an
ambulance siren broke eerily into the stillness. 'Here
they come!' she said grimly. 'We'll just have to do
what we can, and hope the flying doctor won't be too
long getting here. Jerry—he's the ambulance driver—
said on the radio that at least two are critical and will
need to be flown to Adelaide, but probably they'll all
go. They're not locals.' She shook her head worriedly.
'If they're so bad, how they'll have got them all in one
ambulance I don't know.'

Forgetting everything else for the moment, Andie
offered automatically, 'Can I help? Er—you didn't say
your name.'

'Reba. Reba Luscombe.' The nurse's eyes darted
speculatively over Andie and she said doubtfully,
'Look, you're just arrived. . .it's hardly fair. . .'

'I might as well do something as sit around.' As
Andie faced the anxious nurse, the fact that she felt
bone-weary and wasn't planning to stay anyway was
irrelevant. She knew only too well what it meant to
have a crisis on your hands when you were short of
staff.

Reba hesitated only for a moment. 'Well, we could
do with another pair of hands. We're short-staffed as
always—of course you know that, that's why you're
here—and today Matron's off and my senior, Marion,
is sick. Sunday isn't the best day for an emergency!'
She paused as though weighing her options. 'You've
had theatre experience, haven't you?'

Andie nodded. 'Yes.'

Reba looked her over again quickly. 'You must be
dead beat driving all that way. Would you like to take

a shower? I'll chuck you a uniform. I expect Cam will
want all the help we can give him.'

'Cam?' Andie heard herself querying the name in a
whisper. She did not want to reveal that she knew him.

Reba was too preoccupied to notice anything amiss.
'Dr Walters—terrific guy. You'll get along like a house
on fire with him, everyone does. And he's gorgeous
with it! We're lucky. He's a good surgeon, so we don't
have to send so many routine cases to Gawler or even
Adelaide. He wasn't too pleased being called in,
though. He had to fly down from Marshall's Creek,
but Cam would never let anyone down in an emergency. Not like some I could mention,' she added,
tight-lipped.

As she was talking, she ushered Andie to a bathroom along the corridor. 'I'll just get you a towel,' she
said. 'When you've finished, keep straight on down
this corridor. You'll find someone, probably me!' She
grinned. 'Must dash before Cam starts screaming for
me.' She squeezed Andie's arm. 'Thanks a million,
Andie.' Then she was gone.

Andie stripped and stepped into the shower, smiling
to herself. Would anybody in this country ever call her
by her correct name? Until she was twenty she had
always been Andrea, but then along had come Paul
and he'd called her Andie. And when she'd started
nursing in Australia, she'd told everyone her name was
Andrea, but what did they call her? Andie. She hadn't
liked the masculine sound of it at first, but she'd grown
used to it. Australians just couldn't seem to use a
person's proper name, they automatically shortened it.
It was just friendly, Paul had told her, showed you
were accepted.

Well, she'd been accepted here all right, she thought
as the cool water sprayed off her shoulders, revitalising
her tired body. It was going to make it all the harder
to tell them she wasn't staying. Except that she was

bound to have an ally in Cam. He wouldn't want her here. He wouldn't try to keep her.

She dressed in the lightweight pale blue cotton uniform which Reba had flung over a chair with a big towel while she was in the shower, and refused to let herself think about the ordeal ahead. Reba was expecting her to assist Cam, but what would he think about that? That the patients came first, she knew. Whatever his private feelings about her, Cam was a doctor, and he would not let personal animosity interfere with patient care. Andie screwed her pale gold hair into a tighter knot at the back of her head and jabbed the pins in with some fervour. She glanced in the mirror and her large brown eyes looked back uneasily.

It was barely ten minutes after she had entered the bathroom when she emerged, feeling remarkably refreshed. She hurried along the corridor, catching glimpses of wards through half-open doors and, thankfully, she saw Reba coming towards her again.

'What's the situation?' Andie asked, noting the nurse's grave expression.

Reba shook her head slowly. 'Grim, I'm afraid. Two kids unconscious, both with head injuries. Not wearing seatbelts, can you believe? One adult has chest injuries, one has multiple fractures—they were in the car, and an elderly woman has a ruptured spleen and a broken leg. Her husband died on the way here. They were in the car towing the caravan. He had a heart attack, which may have been the cause of the accident. No one's been able to tell us or the police anything yet.'

Andie felt the familiar sick feeling that made her stomach feel as though it was lined with lead whenever she encountered bad accident victims. It was always accompanied by an unreasoning anger. It was usually so senseless. . . But not this time, perhaps. Anyone could have a heart attack. It was just bad luck another vehicle had been coming on just that stretch of lonely road.

'What do you want me to do?' she asked.

'You'd better come and see Cam.'

Andie felt amazingly calm. Her nursing training, as it was meant to, always overrode any personal feelings. She walked into the operating-room behind Reba, and when Cam turned from the patient on the table to look at them—at her—she was amazed at the way she was able to distance herself from knowing him. He stared blankly at her, then his eyes flickered with momentarily surprised recognition, but nothing more.

Reba said in a quiet voice, 'Andie Somers, Cam. She's our new sister. She's just arrived—in the nick of time, wouldn't you say? She's experienced in Theatre.'

Cam glanced back at the male patient, gave Andie another long look, then turned to Reba. 'What's the news on the air ambulance?' he asked.

'On the way.'

Impersonally, Cam's dark eyes snapped back to Andie's face. 'You'd better scrub,' he told her. 'We've got some urgent work to do that can't wait until the patients get to Adelaide. A tracheostomy on this one, for a start.' He directed his attention back to Reba. 'You'd better keep your eye on the others in case I need to alter priorities. Unfortunately, I can only treat one at a time. I'll do the splenectomy next.'

His calm was awesome. From his voice, his manner, Andie thought, no one would have guessed that five people under his care were fighting for their lives. One part of her reacted against his unhurried acceptance of the situation, but she recognised this feeling as panic, and stepped firmly on it. More haste, less speed, her brain reminded her, as a senior tutor at St Catherine's had many times during her training.

She met Cam's gaze with professional detachment. Whatever her personal feelings about him, she knew instinctively that he was the kind of man in whom

patients and medical staff alike put their trust, and
were never disappointed. Only a faint resentment of
this fact lingered as she obeyed the order to scrub up.
Having done so and, with the help of a nurse who said
her name was Vicky, changed into green theatre gown
and cap, and donned mask and gloves, she returned to
the operating-room where another nurse was now also
assisting.

'I'm Lenore,' the girl whispered. She looked scared.
'I—I've only recently qualified. Is this all right?' She
looked at the instrument tray she had set up as though
the scalpels might jump up and cut her to pieces.

Andie checked the tray and smiled. 'Fine. I think
you've got everything he'll need there.' She looked
closely at the girl. 'You've never seen anything quite
so traumatic before?'

Lenore shook her head. Her lip trembled and a tear
ran down her cheek. Andie remembered vividly her
first encounter with really serious injuries and death,
and felt a wave of sympathy. 'You'll be OK,' she
whispered. 'Think of it as a learning experience.'

The young nurse gave her a faint but brave smile.

'Andie, give me a hand, will you?' Cam's brisk tones
galvanised Andie into action. For the next few minutes
not a thought entered her head apart from concentrat-
ing on passing whatever instruments Cam asked for,
and carefully monitoring the general condition of the
patient. She watched closely as Cam made the opening
through the upper rings of the trachea, close to the
skin surface, and inserted the tracheostomy tube which
would facilitate the man's breathing while the injury to
his throat and neck was dealt with. She could not help
but admire his skilled performance.

The sense of urgency in the operating-room was
palpable, but Cam showed the least sign of it. He
spoke quietly and worked steadily, without rush or
fuss, to make sure that the victims of the road smash
would be able to travel safely and comfortably to a

larger hospital which could provide all the facilities to
give them the very best of medical care. His green
gown was splashed with blood and despite the air-
conditioning there was a tell-tale damp rim around the
edge of his cap. Almost at the moment he had done all
he could for the patients, a nurse came to tell them
that the flying doctor had arrived.

'About bloody time!' Cam muttered with feeling,
the first show of emotion Andie had seen from him.

'Will the plane be able to take all of them?' Andie
asked.

'It better be,' he said, and for a moment their eyes
met, his cold and steady. Andie looked quickly away,
busying herself with the drip stand she had set up
beside the patient.

At his request, she went with Cam to help transfer
the accident victims from the ambulance to the aircraft.
Boobera airfield was only two minutes from the hospital and the transfer was done with speed and efficiency,
and few words, except between Cam and the doctor
and sister who had come with the air ambulance.
Andie felt a special pang when she helped ease the
two children, both still unconscious, into the cabin
where their stretchers, like the rest, were strapped
down. Those ashen faces with their oxygen masks and
drips looked so still, so lifeless. But she had felt the
faintly fluttering pulses herself and knew they had a
chance. She crossed her fingers as the aircraft door
closed.

In minutes, the plane was airborne. Cam's face was
taut with strain and anxiety as he watched.

'You did all you could,' Andie said gently. He just
stared at her for a moment, saying nothing. In the
glare of the bright sunlight, she was acutely aware of
the fine lines around his eyes, the deeper ones framing
his mouth, and, in a sudden rush of feeling that
shocked her, an urge to smooth them away. She had
often felt keenly the stress doctors, especially sur-

geons, suffered and sympathised with them, but this
was unexpected. She didn't even like this man.

'You'd better go back with the ambulance,' Cam
said abruptly. 'Tell Reba I'll be in shortly.'

He marched over to his Range Rover, and Andie
joined the ambulance crew, who, now that the crisis
was over, were full of jokes, and curious about her.
She was too weary to tell them that she wasn't going
to be the new nurse after all.

Reba hurried to greet her on their arrival back at
the hospital. 'You must be ready to collapse. How
about a nice cup of tea?'

The tension which had been holding Andie together
eased, and her limbs seemed to turn to jelly. 'And a
sit-down,' she said. 'I feel—wobbly.'

'You did a great job,' Reba praised. 'I don't know
what we'd have done without you.'

'Coped,' said Andie with a smile. 'Nurses always do,
don't they?'

Reba laughed. 'Come into my office. Cup of tea
first—and maybe a little of something for medicinal
purposes—then we'll straighten out a few details
before we settle you in.'

Andie bit her lip. She still hadn't come up with an
excuse for not staying that didn't sound ridiculous.
Maybe she should tell Reba the truth. She balked at
that, but perhaps it was the only way. Reba seemed an
understanding person.

Hot sweet tea with a tot of brandy in a medicine
glass was Reba's recipe for the shock she insisted
Andie had suffered. Reba was going to get a shock of
a different kind, Andie thought, steeling herself to tell
the nurse she wasn't staying.

'Reba——' she began hesitantly, but was interrupted by the telephone.

She looked out of the window on to the green lawns
surrounding the hospital. The shadows were lengthening. She would have to spend the night in Boobera

whether she liked it or not, as it was getting too late to start driving back to Adelaide. She didn't like driving at night in strange territory, especially country as remote and lonely as this.

Reba put the phone down and looked up, but not at Andie, over her shoulder. Andie automatically glanced round and saw Cam in the doorway. He looked weary, and there were tension lines still grooving his mouth and brow. He was good-looking, Andie thought, in an arrogant sort of way. And she had to hand it to him—he knew his job. He'd worked furiously to make sure there was nothing more that could have been done for those RTA victims, to ensure that their chances of survival were optimum.

'I'm off,' he said to Reba.

'You're flying back?'

'No, it's hardly worth it. The weekend's almost over.'

The nurse nodded. 'You could take tomorrow off.'

He shook his head. 'Can't. I've got two tonsillectomies in the morning and Mrs Garrett's sebaceous cyst.'

Reba eyed him sympathetically. 'They could wait.'

He was adamant. 'As I'm down here I might as well stay.' A faint smile drifted across his mouth but did not quite obscure the lines of strain there. He included Andie in his glance as he said, 'Broken weekends is just one of the hazards of our profession.'

Reba said, 'I was going to take Andie along to the annexe later, but as you're here. . .'

Cam looked at Andie. 'Sure. She can come with me.' His gaze gave away nothing.

Reba turned to Andie. 'You look dead on your feet,' she said bluntly. 'Go with Cam and we'll talk about rosters and all that tomorrow. Come in when you feel like it—no rush. I don't suppose we'll have another day like today. I hope!'

The phone rang again, and Lenore hovered in the doorway, obviously anxious to speak to Reba.

Cam said brusquely, 'Come on, Andie.' He strode off along the corridor and Andie hurried after him.

As she caught up with him in the car park, she blurted out, 'Cam. . .obviously I—I can't stay. . .'

He stopped and turned to look at her. 'Why not?'

'No. . . No, I couldn't.' She bit her lip hard. 'You can't want me to. It's embarrassing for both of us.'

'Is it? I'm not embarrassed.' He paused meaningfully. 'But I guess you've got plenty of reason to be.'

Andie clenched her fists. 'Cam, I don't want to discuss it. I'll go to a hotel tonight and leave in the morning.'

'And what'll you tell Reba? Or will you just run out on us?' His lips curled sarcastically as though it was only to be expected of her.

'No! I'll tell her. I'll think of something. . .'

His gaze was hard, cold and reminded her of that terrible last time in London when he'd castigated her so cruelly.

'Reba works her feet off,' he said quietly. 'She's been trying to get an extra nurse for months, and you're not even that, just a replacement. It's not easy to get staff in country hospitals, especially ones as isolated as Boobera. She'll be devastated if you chicken out. Now you're here, you might as well stay.'

Andie coloured. 'I just thought you'd probably rather. . .'

'I don't care one way or the other,' he said. He looked hard at her. 'Think about it. If you still want to go in the morning, go, but don't go because of me. You obviously chose this job for some good reason. The fact that we happen to have known each other in rather less than amicable circumstances needn't be a problem.' He added pointedly, 'Why *did* you choose to take a job in the outback? You're a city girl. I thought you hated the country. Like Paul.' His eyes dropped to her bare left hand. 'You're not married?' He sounded surprised.

'No.' She asked carefully, 'D—does Paul ever come up here?'

Cam's eyebrows rose and his lips curved cynically, showing his strong white teeth. 'Paul? Come here? You have to be joking. He'd freak out in a place like this. If you're afraid he might suddenly appear to embarrass you, don't be. He won't. And believe me, I won't tell him you're here. I rarely see him anyway.' There was a trace of bitterness in his tone.

Andie moistened her lips. 'I think I'd still rather leave,' she said.

He cocked an eyebrow derisively. 'Still selfish, aren't you? What you want always comes first, doesn't it?'

'That's not. . .' She took a deep breath and swallowed her retort. His eyes challenged her until she heard herself say, 'All right, I'll sleep on it. If you could just direct me to where I'm to stay, this annexe or whatever it is.'

'It's a small bungalow in the grounds of my house.'

This announcement sent a shock wave through her.

Cam explained, 'It was built by the former owners for an elderly relative. I've been using it as an office and storage space, but as the board is refurbishing the nurses' accommodation, and those who need to be have been billeted out for a couple of months, I offered the annexe until the renovating is finished.'

'Would you still have done so if you'd known *I* was coming?'

He shrugged. 'That's irrelevant.'

His apparent indifference was getting under Andie's skin, and she didn't know what to say, but she was thinking that now more than ever she would have to leave in the morning. She couldn't possibly work with Cam *and* live in proximity to him. For tonight she had no choice but to stay in the annexe. She knew what he would say if she suggested a hotel.

'Let's get going,' he said. 'Just follow along behind—

it's only a few minutes away.' He laughed. 'It's a bit hard to get lost in Boobera.'

He headed for the Range Rover and seemed to notice for the first time that she had moved her car. When they'd dashed to the airfield, there hadn't been time to notice anything. He shot her a mildly puzzled look. 'I told you there was no need to move. And that's hardly a sensible position.'

Andie felt a fool. 'I—I'm afraid I ran out of gas. I must have only just made it here.'

He looked from her to her car, which faced the entrance, and back again. 'You would have turned tail and run if your tank hadn't been empty?'

Andie's face flushed scarlet, but she had to brave it out. 'Is there somewhere I can get some petrol? I don't suppose you've got a can. . .'

For a moment he looked as though he wanted to laugh. If he did, she thought, she'd swipe him. 'No, I haven't. Let's get your luggage and I'll give you a lift.'

'No!'

He glowered at her. 'Yes! Look, Andie, I'm whacked. For that matter, so are you. The sooner we get home and get some rest the better. Standing about here arguing isn't a great help. I'll get someone to fill your tank, don't worry, and drive the car round to my place in the morning.'

He flipped open the boot and lifted out her two suitcases. 'This all you've got?'

'And a holdall.' She fetched it from the back of the car, and meekly followed him back to the Range Rover. This was bizarre. If she'd had the slightest inkling. . . She heaved a sigh as she got in beside him. There was no way she was going to stay, no way at all. Whatever Reba might think of her, whatever Cam thought of her, however much she hated herself for letting them down, she wasn't going to stay in Boobera. Not with Cam there. It was impossible. Tomorrow she was leaving. Definitely.

CHAPTER TWO

'Do you like Chinese?'

Cam's voice startled Andie. As she had climbed into the Range Rover beside him, the past had come flooding back with a vengeance, submerging her. The hospital gates were a blur as he drove through, and even the brilliant sunset over the purple ranges beyond the tiny outback town barely caught her notice.

'I beg your pardon?' She glanced at him. The shock of dark hair which had been flattened under the slouch hat and later his theatre cap was now springing up and bouncing forward on to his forehead, just the way she remembered. At their first meeting she had been amused because, in a grey suit and old school tie, he had looked so suave, so sophisticated, so much the formidable professional that Paul had told her he was—except for his appealingly unruly hair. Now why would she remember that? Because she remembered just about everything about him, she realised. He was such a physical man, he made such an impact. And she'd had good reason to have every detail about him stamped on her memory.

'I said do you like Chinese food?' A raised eyebrow underlined the query.

Andie forced herself to get a grip on reality. They were cruising along the main street of Boobera, with its verandaed shops, balconied hotel and an air of being as deserted as a ghost town.

'Er—yes, I do,' she said. It was good of him, she supposed, to think of the fact that she would need an evening meal.

'Only place open on a Sunday,' he explained. 'We'll stop and get something.'

21

He drove another half-block, then pulled in to the kerb and dragged on the handbrake. Andie fumbled for her purse and followed him into the take-away restaurant. He wouldn't let her pay for hers, and, faced with his hard-set mouth, she didn't argue too much.

They drove the rest of the way in silence, and she was glad that it was no longer than five minutes. Cam parked the Range Rover in his driveway, in front of a sprawling weatherboard house with wide verandas covered in grapevines. He lifted her cases out of the vehicle and jerked his head towards the side of the house.

'This way.'

Andie, juggling her holdall, handbag and the Chinese take-away packages, stumbled after him down a gravel path between shrubberies of mixed native and exotic plants. Just beyond the back of the house, and tucked away amid trees and tall shrubs, was a small timber building which Andie presumed, rightly, was the annexe.

Cam put her cases down on the tiny front porch and fitted a key in the door. He threw the door open and marched inside, leaving her to trail along behind.

'There you are,' he said. 'It's not a bad set-up. You have your own kitchen and bathroom, and there's parking space for your car out the front.' The dark eyebrows twitched a fraction. 'Just don't block my way in or out, will you?'

Andie went pink. 'No. . .' She glanced around. 'Thanks. It's very nice.' The green and pale yellow tonings of the furnishings were cool and soothing, sunny but soft. She didn't even have to look closely to know that everything would be spotlessly clean. There was a faint aroma of eucalyptus on the air.

Cam marched into the kitchen. 'Fridge is on.' He opened the door. 'Jean's left you milk and eggs and a few other things, by the look of it.' He enlightened her. 'Jean Barlow is my housekeeper.'

'That's very kind of her. Please thank her for me.'

Cam gave her a sideways glance. 'You can thank her yourself in due course—that is, if you stay.'

Andie bit her lip. There was no question; she wasn't staying. She dumped the take-away meal on the kitchen table. 'Which was yours?' she murmured, fumbling with the wrappings. His hand on her shoulder made her turn her head to look up at him in alarm.

He dropped his hand. 'We'll share if you like. Any objection if I eat with you?'

She was surprised. She'd thought he would have wanted to leave her to her own devices. 'No, of course not.' But she wished he hadn't suggested it. He unnerved her, made her feel edgy and uncomfortable. 'I thought you would have rather. . .'

'Eaten alone? Is that what you'd rather do?'

Andie ran her tongue nervously over her bottom lip. 'Your housekeeper's not home this evening?'

'No. She's in Adelaide for the weekend.' He waited a moment, then moved decisively towards the bench near the stove. 'I'll put the kettle on,' he said. 'I dare say Jean's left you tea and coffee.' He opened a cupboard. 'Yep, here we are. Which would you prefer?'

'Tea, please.'

'Plates are in that cupboard there,' he said, pointing.

Andie fetched out plates and unwrapped their food. Cam made a pot of tea and they sat at the kitchen table to eat the meal. Andie couldn't help remembering the one and only other time she'd had a meal with Cam, that night Paul had introduced her to his brother, when they'd dined at a posh restaurant in London and she'd known straight away that Cam was not going to approve of her. The way he'd looked at her then, tight-lipped, disdainful, derogating her without even saying a word, wasn't so far from the way he was

looking at her now. It made her blood heat rise now
as it had then.

'I thought you were tired,' she said, attacking her
fried rice and vegetables with the chopsticks.

'I am.' He tilted his chair back, observing her from
under lowered lids. 'I shan't stay long, don't worry. As
soon as I've had this I'll dive into the house and crash.
As I dare say you will too.'

'There's nothing surer.' Andie stifled a yawn, and
took a gulp of tea. Her eyelids were heavy. The day's
stresses and strains were rapidly catching up with her.

Cam regarded her silently for a moment, then said,
'Thanks for mucking in today. You did a great job.'

'I only did what was necessary.' She added, 'I
gathered from what you and Reba were saying that
you'd had to come back from somewhere. Were you
very far away?'

He didn't seem to mind her curiosity. 'No. I have a
property in the Flinders Ranges, a former cattle
station. I bought it a couple of years ago, as a retreat,
I suppose you could say. I liked it so much I decided
to live up here permanently. I go there as often as I
can.'

Andie was intrigued. 'But you had a very good job
in Sydney.'

He nodded, smiling. 'I'm just as useful up in this
neck of the woods. Anyway, I was becoming too much
of an administrator down there.'

'But you're so well qualified. . .' she couldn't help
saying.

'Do the people who live in Boobera and the surrounding district deserve less qualified medical care?'

'No, of course not, but—well, they can be transferred to big city hospitals when necessary,' Andie
pointed out. 'As happened today.'

'That's true, but sometimes they don't want to go,
can't afford to be away too long—there are all kinds
of reasons why it's better on occasions to treat patients

right here. Within the limits of our resources and
equipment, of course, which naturally are not compar-
able with city hospital high tech! But we have a very
active fund-raising committee which has financed most
of our equipment.'

'And like today, I suppose someone with your
experience can save lives while you're waiting for the
flying doctor to arrive,' Andie conceded.

He shrugged. 'Perhaps that's the case sometimes.'

She was still curious. 'Reba said you flew—does that
mean you have your own plane?'

He nodded. 'I have a nice little Cessna four-seater.'
He paused, eyeing her speculatively. 'There's no need
to look impressed—a lot of people fly themselves
around in this country. I'll have to take you for a run
up to Marshall's Creek some time. If you stay, of
course,' he added, perhaps regretting his rash
invitation.

Andie flinched. His eyes were challenging her
openly again. 'What do you do there?' she asked,
evading the issue. 'Hunting, shooting and fishing, I
suppose.'

His expression was shocked. 'Good God, no! Those
pursuits are precisely the ones which are banned on
my property. It's a wildlife sanctuary.' His eyes narrowed. 'I trust you haven't any inclinations to blast
your fellow creatures to bits for pleasure, or to torture
them with fish-hooks?'

'Definitely not.' Andie was pleased that her assumption was wrong. It was heartening to make such a
discovery about Cameron Walters, and unexpected.
She felt herself momentarily warming towards him in
spite of her deep antagonism.

'I'm pleased to hear it.' Cam was watching her
intently. 'Unfortunately, there are a lot of people who
take great pleasure in shooting wallabies, and 'roos,
even in a sanctuary, and we have endless trouble
catching them and even more trying to prosecute them.

My ranger has his work cut out at certain times keeping track of what's going on. Marshall's Creek covers a few hundred thousand hectares.'

'It sounds very remote and wild,' Andie said.

He laughed derisively. 'It's no place for a raw little Pommie! At least Boobera has faint trappings of civilisation. Marshall's Creek is like being on top of the world, or as someone said recently, after seeing some of our scenery, on the moon. I think a day trip would be enough for you, Andie.'

She bridled at his derogatory tone. 'I've been in Australia for five years, Cam. Who knows? I might even get to like the outback,' she said.

He looked sceptical and taunted, 'If you stay!'

He was challenging her again, and she felt nettled. She bent her head and concentrated on her food for a minute or two.

Cam swallowed the last mouthful of his, and pushed the plate away. He topped up his tea, then said slowly, 'Andie, there's no need to make my being here the reason for chucking in this job before you've even started. Just treat it as an unfortunate coincidence.'

Andie could feel her hair coming down and fumbled with a clip. 'Don't you think it will make working together difficult?' she asked.

'Why should it? It wasn't me you married.' His eyes narrowed, the lids drooping heavily, wearily. 'I can't help it that things turned out rather as I predicted. But what's done is done. Of course, if your conscience is what's making you reluctant. . .'

'My conscience is clear!'

His scathing look infuriated her. What did she have to feel guilty about?

He shrugged and their eyes locked briefly before she dragged hers away.

'It seems a pity to have come all this way, only to turn round and go back,' he said. Then, arching one eyebrow, 'Why *did* you come to this godforsaken spot, Andie? What were you escaping from?'

Andie wasn't about to tell him—Paul. 'I wanted a change, that's all.' It didn't sound convincing, and she felt sure he wasn't convinced. 'I thought it was time I saw something of the outback.' She went on boldly, 'You're the last person I'd have expected to find here. I thought *you* were very much a city person.'

He was amused. 'You never had a chance to discover much about me, did you?'

'You never gave me one!'

'No, I suppose I did treat you a little high-handedly. But only with your best interests at heart, Andie. Yours and Paul's.'

'There's no point in apologising now,' she said tightly. 'That's easy to do when you've been proved right.'

'That really galls you, doesn't it?'

'No, it doesn't!' Andie could hear herself getting shrill. She was tired, her nerves on edge, and she wished he'd go and leave her alone. She didn't want to discuss Paul and the failure of their marriage. She wanted to forget. 'If you've finished. . .well, I'd like to. . .' She was faltering now, her brain refusing to cope. Fatigue was catching up with her like jet lag.

'Get some rest. Sure.' He stood up. 'See you tomorrow. Like Reba said, don't rush. No need for you to appear on deck at dawn.'

'But—I won't be. . .' she murmured, slurring her words as though she had been drinking something stronger than tea. She looked at him, looming over her, and his face began to blur. It was becoming painful to keep her eyes open.

He bent towards her and tilted her chin with strong fingers. She inhaled a faint whiff of antiseptic, and, as though it was ether, she closed her eyes. She heard Cam say musingly, 'Whatever else you are, Andie, I never thought you were a coward.'

Whether she answered, she never knew. Tiredness
won and she slumped forward, her head on her folded
arms. She didn't feel him lift her and carry her into the
bedroom, turn back the covers, lay her down gently
and pull off her shoes and uniform. She was already
dead to the world.

Andie woke in a wide beam of sunshine that dazzled
so much that she couldn't see where she was. Sleep
still hung heavily on her and it was some moments
before she shook it off and sat up. She was not at first
surprised to find herself in her bra and panties. She
had been so tired last night. . . And then as the room
came into focus and memory flipped up images, she
felt her skin tingle with heat that was nothing to do
with the heat of the day.

It was cool in the room and she could hear the
whirring of an air-conditioner somewhere in the house.
She swung her feet to the floor and stood up. Her eyes
alighted on her two suitcases parked neatly side by
side just inside the bedroom door. She hadn't even
unpacked her toilet gear.

The last thing she remembered was saying something
to Cam at the kitchen table. She must have fallen
asleep, and he must have carried her into the bedroom,
removed her shoes and uniform and laid her on the
bed. How could she have been unaware? How could
she have let him do that without protest? She went hot
and cold again at the thought.

It was nine o'clock. She had slept for nearly twelve
hours. She unzipped a suitcase and dragged out a
cotton dressing-gown. She went to the window to draw
the blind against the sun and looked out between the
net curtains on to a patio area under a pergola festooned with a creeper with bright yellow flowers.

Barefoot, she padded into the hallway, and found a
sitting room opposite the bedroom. The window here
looked up the pathway to the front of Cam's house,

but the view was almost entirely obscured by shrubbery. There was no sign of her car, but if Cam had asked someone to bring it round, as he'd promised, she wouldn't be able to see where it was parked from here. If she could, she mused with a smile, it would be blocking his way in or out!

Well, she couldn't go and look dressed like this. The first thing to do was have a shower and dress. And then she'd better ring Reba and try to explain her change of mind.

She unpacked a pair of pink cotton pedal-pushers and a white T-shirt and laid them on the bed with clean underwear. Then she took a shower and dressed. She wandered into the kitchen to make a cup of tea, not admitting that she was looking for ways to postpone ringing the hospital for as long as possible.

But it couldn't be put off for ever. She sat at the kitchen table, twisting strands of blonde hair into ringlets while staring into her teacup and trying to concoct a convincing reason for going. 'Letting them down' was how Cam would put it. 'I never thought you were a coward'. That was the last thing he'd said, she remembered suddenly.

'If only he weren't here,' she said aloud. 'I'm sure I could get to like the place, if only *he* weren't here.' He'd been pleasant enough to her last night, but she knew that underneath that veneer of politeness he despised her. Maybe he'd been putting on an act last night too, hoping she'd change her mind and stay, so he could make life miserable for her by reminding her constantly that he'd been right about Paul's and her marriage. Or maybe he had just been thinking of Reba, short-staffed and overworked, and who, if Andie went, would have to start all over again trying to get a nurse who wanted to work in the outback.

'Damn you, Cameron Walters,' she muttered. 'Why couldn't you have stayed at Sydney's Southern Cross Hospital instead of burying yourself in the very town where I decide to take a job?' Fate could be a cruel trickster.

She poured a second cup of tea, and the telephone rang. She grimaced. She could hardly pretend she wasn't there. If this was Cam. . . Apprehensively, she ran into the hall and lifted the receiver.

'Hello,' she said.

'Good morning!' It was Reba. 'How are you feeling?'

'Fine, thanks.' Tell her, Andie's brain urged. Go on, tell her.

'I thought you might have surfaced by now,' Reba went on cheerfully. 'But I'm not hassling you. We're pretty quiet at the moment. I just called to say if you want to go and do some shopping for food and such-like, go ahead, and drop by this afternoon. Settle yourself in first. Cam's fixed up about your car. Old Mack, the groundsman, is getting her tank filled, and he'll be bringing her round any minute. If you could just drop him back?'

'Reba, I. . .' Andie faltered.

But Reba heard no hesitation in her tone. She went on, 'Actually, it would be great if you could turn up straight after lunch. Cam's got two ops today.'

'I thought they were this morning,' Andie remembered.

'He put them both off until this afternoon. He said seeing we've got an experienced theatre nurse on the premises again we might as well make good use of you.' Reba laughed in a relieved kind of way. 'He's been like a bear with a sore head since Val left us. I never manage to please him completely, but evidently you did everything just the way he likes it. Don't worry, it's not sour grapes—I'm just relieved. Theatre isn't my first love, and you can teach Lenore and the others more than I can. Look, why don't you do your grocery shopping and then come and have lunch in the canteen? You can meet the rest of the staff and

Matron, and then scrub for Cam this afternoon. He reckons on starting about two-thirty.'

Andie took a deep breath. It was now or never. If she was going to leave, she had to say so now. As she opened her mouth to deliver her excuses, lame though they might sound, there was a knock at the door.

'There's someone at the door,' she said instead.

'That'll be Mack,' said Reba confidently. 'You'd better go. I'll expect you about twelve, OK? Got to go myself—Lenore's in a panic again! And by the way, you left your clothes here yesterday.'

Andie heard the receiver disconnect them and gave a sigh of frustration. The knocking at her door came again.

'I'm coming!' she yelled, putting her own receiver down.

An elderly man wearing a large squatter's hat and dungarees grinned at her. 'Sister Somers? I brought your car.'

'Oh—thank you,' Andie said breathlesssly. 'Thanks very much. That was kind of you. What do I owe you for the petrol?'

He doffed his hat. 'Nothing. I was told to put it on Dr Walters's account, miss.'

Andie clenched her teeth. 'I see. Oh, well, I'll see him about it. Thanks again for driving the car round for me. I'll take you back to the hospital. Hang on a second while I get my bag.'

Now, she thought, she would have to go in and see Reba and explain face to face. Well, perhaps that was more honest than doing it over the telephone. Besides, she had to collect her clothes and return the uniform. When she came back, Mack was slumped against the door-frame, and his breathing was alarmingly irregular.

'Are you all right?' Andie asked anxiously.

He thumped the palm of his hand against his chest. 'Fine, just fine—I get these pains sometimes. Nothing

to worry about. Just angina.' He staggered a little as
he set off back along the path, and Andie frowned.
His colour hadn't looked good to her. She locked the
door and ran after him. His breathing was even more
laboured after the exertion, and she was sure he
needed medical attention. Just as well they were going
to the hospital. 'Have you taken any medication?' she
asked.

He nodded. 'One of me pills.'

'Anginine?'

He flipped it on to the end of his tongue and showed
her.

'Good.' Relieved, she helped him into the car and
went around to the driver's seat. He was still clutching
his chest. Thank goodness it was only five minutes to
the hospital. She hoped she could remember the way.

Mack seemed to sense her hesitation. 'Go to the end
of this street,' he rasped, speaking now with some
difficulty. 'And turn right. A coupla hundred yards
and you'll be on the main road. Straight through town
and it's first turning on the left.'

'Yes. I remember that bit from yesterday,' Andie
said, pulling away from the kerb. She added, 'I think
you ought to see the doctor.'

'Maybe I'd better. . .' the old man conceded, his
head sinking on to his chest. 'I'm getting this pain in
me chest and arms more often lately. . .'

Andie drove fast, cornering with a squeal of brakes,
but there was no traffic to speak of, and so far as she
could see no speed-limit apart from the signs at either
end of the town where the main street became the
highway. She pulled up as close to the hospital's
Casualty entrance as she could and flew inside.

There was no one in Reception. Andie sped along
the corridor to Cam's office, and was about to burst in
when his voice hailed her from behind.

'What's the panic?'

She wheeled round. 'Oh, thank goodness, I'm so

glad you're here. I've got the gardener—Mack—out in my car. I'm afraid he might be having a heart attack.' She added quickly, 'He's taken anginine, but it doesn't seem to be having any effect. He says he's been having the pains more often lately.'

Cam didn't waste time on words. With lightning speed, the old gardener was transferred to a stretcher and carried into the hospital. Andie wasn't required to help; there were other nurses today to do Cam's bidding.

Andie found herself sitting in Reba's office, waiting until the senior sister could see her. A young nurse who introduced herself as Jessica brought her a cup of tea.

'You're having exciting times!' she teased. 'Two emergencies in two days, and you've only just arrived. I hope you haven't jinxed the place.'

Andie laughed. 'So do I!' As the nurse seemed inclined to linger, she added, 'How long have you been here, Jessica?'

Jessica perched on the edge of the desk. 'Two years, and I love it—really. It's a great place to work. Everyone's so friendly and nice, and the town's really great too. They think a lot of us here, not like some places where they take you for granted. I wouldn't be leaving if I didn't have to.'

'You're leaving?' Andie asked.

The girl blushed. 'Yes—I'm getting married. But I haven't told anyone I'm engaged yet. My fiancé works in Adelaide and we plan to marry soon, but you wouldn't believe how hard it is to tell them. I keep meaning to and then I get cold feet. It was awful when Val left. I'm glad they got someone at last.' She grinned at Andie. 'You don't know how delighted I was to see you! I'm definitely going to tell Reba today. I know it means they'll be short-staffed again, but at least it won't be quite so bad as Val and me both going and no replacements.'

Andie listened to her with growing dismay. She felt as though tentacles were wrapping themselves around her, and there was no escape. But it wasn't her fault Jessica wanted to leave. They must be able to get someone else. . .

Jessica left her, and shortly afterwards Reba came in.

'How is the old man?' Andie asked at once.

'He'll be OK. You got him here just in time. He's had a couple of attacks before. You know what he was doing? Using anginine over two years old! No wonder it was having no effect. He said he didn't want to waste them. We'll have to keep him in for a week or two this time.' Reba laughed resignedly. 'We'll have to find someone else to do the gardening for a bit!' She said teasingly, 'Must have been the excitement of filling up the new nurse's car and delivering it. You'll have to watch old Mack!' Her smile slipped a little and she added in a rather tense tone, 'I might as well warn you that there's someone else here you'll need to watch.'

Andie was startled. 'Cam. . .?'

'Heavens, no! He's not interested in nurses! He's practically engaged to the woman who owns the property next door to his, a well-off young widow who runs her place as a tourist resort, and Madeleine is one sexy lady. No, Cam's not a problem. I mean Barry, our visiting medico and resident flirt, Dr Barry Lester. He's in partnership with Dr Warrington, the local GP. Probably won't last long in this neck of the woods, though, which might be a good thing.'

The slightly wistful expression in Reba's eyes made Andie wonder if Reba was more than a little under the spell of the flirtatious Dr Lester, and suffering for it.

'Just thought I'd mention it,' Reba said quickly. She gave Andie an apologetic look. 'I hope I'm not putting you off. I wouldn't want to lose you too soon. I know Boobera isn't everyone's cup of tea, but it does grow on you, and there's a lot more social activity than you'd think. They're really nice people here. I suppose I shouldn't really say that, being local myself.'

'Jessica was telling me she loves it here,' said Andie. 'She brought me a cup of tea.'

'She's a good girl. Pity she's leaving.'

'Oh, she told you, then?'

Reba nodded. 'Just now. She told you too, did she? It means we'll have to look for a replacement again. It's never-ending.' She brushed her hand across her forehead. 'Do try and stick it out for a while, Andie,' she pleaded. 'I don't want to have a nervous breakdown.'

Andie's lip trembled. How could she say she was going now? Panic gripped her. She must go. She couldn't stay.

A nurse came to the office and Reba went out with her, saying she'd be right back. Andie clenched her fingers and steeled herself. When the door opened again, she looked up, determined now to say her piece. But it wasn't Reba who came in, but Dr Walters.

'You slept well, I hope?' he said, examining her with his dark eyes as though she were a recalcitrant patient.

'Very well, thanks.' Andie could hardly bear to look at him. 'By the way, how much do I owe you for the petrol?'

'Nothing. On the house.'

'No. . .' she began.

'I'll add it to your rent,' he said smoothly.

'But I'm not. . .'

The door swung open again and Reba came bustling in. 'Oh, hello, Cam. I was just going to take Andie along to meet Matron. Then she can go and do her shopping, and come back for lunch and meet everyone else.'

Cam gave Andie a long steady look and angled one eyebrow. 'I'm glad you've decided to stay after all, Sister Somers,' he said.

Reba looked frantic. 'You weren't thinking of chucking it in?'

Andie gulped and groped in vain for words.

Cam said, 'She was a little doubtful last night. Yesterday was something of a traumatic experience for all of us, but I assured her that crises like that don't, thank goodness, happen very often.'

Reba was still looking at Andie as though she expected her to vanish into thin air. 'You are staying, Andie, aren't you?'

To Andie, Cam's eyes were accusing and as vocal as speech. Coward. Silly, impetuous girl. Unreasonable to let the past make a difference. Grow up. Stop holding a childish grudge against me. She could have hurled a heavy object at him.

Well, she wasn't a coward, and oddly enough, even considering the circumstances, she did want to stay. She liked what she'd seen of the hospital and the staff so far, and she didn't want to let them down. She didn't want to drive all the way back to Melbourne and start looking for another job. To hell with Cam Walters, she thought suddenly. She wasn't going to run away because of him. She'd stood up to him before, and she would again if need be.

Andie avoided looking at him as she said, 'Of course I am. I was a bit tired last night, not sure I could cope. . .' She raised her eyes to him. With *you*, her gaze emphasised.

'Cope!' exclaimed Reba. 'If anyone can cope, you can, Andie. Right, Cam?'

'Sure,' he said, with faint mockery.

'Phew! Well, that's a relief,' said Reba. 'You had me worried there for a moment. Now, I've got two months to find a replacement for Jessica, that is if no one else quits in the meantime. Maybe it isn't too bad. Come on, Andie, let's go and see Matron.'

CHAPTER THREE

'WELCOME, my dear! I hope you'll stay with us for a nice long time. From what I've heard, we're very lucky to have you. I'm only sorry I wasn't here to help with Sunday's emergency, and you were thrown in at the deep end when you'd scarcely arrived. We're all grateful.'

Embarrassed, Andie shook the hand that Matron Peg Castle extended and felt an instant rapport. She found herself smiling despite the turmoil still churning inside her. Matron Castle's soft West Country accent, together with the warm welcome, had completed her capitulation.

'I really didn't mind,' Andie said. 'An emergency is an emergency.' She added, 'I'm very happy to be here.' Which she was.

She must accept that fate had brought her to Boobera, where the man she least wanted to see again, Cameron Walters, was, and, although she wasn't keen to admit it, some strange compulsion was urging her to see it through. She'd fought against it, but fate had done a great job of taking advantage of her weak will-power and preventing her from running away, and had finally ensured that she accepted the *fait accompli*. Perhaps it was some kind of test, she thought fatalistically.

'You're English!' Peg Castle said, looking as pleased as Andie was to see a fellow-countrywoman.

Reba discreetly withdrew, and Andie spent half an hour in pleasant, nostalgic conversation with the matron. Peg Castle had come to Australia fifteen years before and had not yet been back. Her husband owned the Boobera garage and they had three grown-up

37

children, all married and living in various parts of
Australia. She was eager to talk to someone about
'home'.

'I love this country, and outback folk are the salt of
the earth,' she said, with genuine affection, 'but sometimes I miss the rain, even the fogs, and the *greenness*
of the countryside.' She laughed at herself. 'But only
occasionally. I really love this part of Australia. The
Flinders Ranges scenery is so spectacular, the colours
so vibrant, it takes your breath away. You'll love it,
Andie.'

Eventually the telephone interrupted, and although
Andie was enjoying talking to Matron she was glad to
get away so she could do some shopping and get back
in time for lunch.

The town's only supermarket was small but well
stocked, and Andie was amused to find herself greeted
by name as she entered, by staff and customers alike.
Everyone it seemed already knew about the new nurse,
her part in the previous day's crisis, and that she was
living in the annexe to Dr Walters' house. The realisation that privacy in a small town was likely to be
somewhat limited disturbed her, but she supposed she
would get used to it. And with a bit of luck she might
be only a nine-days' wonder.

When she reached the checkout with her trolley,
Andie realised she had bought rather more than she'd
intended, and it was going to take two trips to transfer
it all to the car, which was parked a short distance
away.

'I'll come back for the rest,' she told the check-out
girl as she took a heavy plastic bag of groceries in each
hand. 'Shan't be long.'

A pleasant male voice said, 'Let me give you a
hand.'

'Oh, hello, Dr Lester,' trilled the check-out girl, and
fluttered long mascaraed lashes at the tall sandy-haired
man who had come up behind Andie.

Andie looked round. 'Thank you. I'm Andrea Somers, the new nurse at the hospital.'

'Yes, I know.' His hazel eyes had a wicked twinkle and Andie recalled Reba's warning. Yes, he was a flirt all right. The look he was giving her right now confirmed that. 'Here, let me take those.' He tried to wrest the bags she was already carrying from her grasp as well as scoop up the remaining two.

'It's all right, I can manage these,' Andie jerked away rather sharply as his hands brushed over hers, deliberately, she was sure. 'My car's only a few steps away.'

Unabashed and still smiling, Dr Lester pushed the store door open for her.

'You had a baptism of fire yesterday, I hear,' he said as they walked to Andie's car.

'I suppose you could say that,' Andie agreed. 'It wasn't quite the welcome I expected.' She halted and dumped her shopping bags on the kerb while she lifted the hatchback.

Dr Lester stowed all the bags in the back for her, then gave her a very thorough visual examination. 'We'll have to organise a more appropriate welcome. How about a party on Saturday night?'

'I'm not sure yet what my shift will be,' Andie prevaricated.

He dismissed any difficulties with a wave of his hand. 'Leave it to me. I expect I can persuade Reba to roster you off on Saturday night.'

Yes, she thought wryly, I expect you can. She wasn't altogether sure she liked this rather self-assured young doctor, but his smile was disarming and his manner cheerful, and she was always willing to reserve judgement.

He wasn't the first young doctor to take more than a passing interest in her physical attributes, but she found such obvious admiration embarrassing, and said hastily, 'I'd better be going. I want to drop this stuff off before I go back to the hospital. I'm supposed to be meeting the rest of the staff over the lunch-hour and starting work this afternoon. Thank you very much for your help, Dr Lester.'

'Barry,' he said. 'We don't stand on ceremony around here.' He opened the car door for her. 'See you later, Andie. Take care.'

Andie drove along the main street, marvelling at the absence of traffic. How wonderful it was not to be stuck in traffic jams, to be irritated by lunatic drivers and dozy pedestrians. What bliss! The town seemed half asleep—not much different from Sunday, she thought, although there were a few people about, shopping in a desultory fashion. It wasn't too hot yet, but the iron roofs of the houses shimmered and the sun from a cloudless sky made shadows sharp and dense.

As she turned into the driveway of Cam's house, Andie's apprehension mounted. How was this going to work out? Practically living with him. She felt a familiar clenching inside as she remembered again his treatment of her five years ago. Her dislike of Paul's brother had not diminished, and even his considerateness last night could not change the way she felt about him. She hoped she was not going to regret letting herself be manipulated into staying.

Having disposed of her groceries, Andie went straight back to the hospital. It was just after midday. During the next hour she met the members of staff who were on duty, and was warmly welcomed by everyone. Reba gave her a tour of the hospital and introduced her to most of the patients.

'Cam is our full-time medico,' Reba explained, 'and Barry and Dr Warrington visit. Barry was on call yesterday, as a matter of fact, but we couldn't locate him, so I had to drag Cam back from Marshall's Creek.' She pulled a face. 'Cam wasn't too pleased, I

can tell you. I've no doubt he'll say a few choice words
to Barry about it.'

'It is a bit irresponsible not to be contactable when
you're on call,' Andie agreed.

'Barry says his beeper wasn't working. I suggested
he get a new one, but he said he'd get it fixed. If you
ask me he just forgot to put new batteries in it. But he
has his good points. He's a whizz at delivering babies,
and he's a favourite with children.' Reba smiled indul-
gently. 'There are no tears when Dr Lester looks at
tonsils and cut feet.'

'So you make allowances.' Andie was sure now that
Reba was very smitten with the flirtatious Dr Lester.
She already liked Reba enough to hope he wouldn't
be irresponsible enough to break her heart.

Reba shrugged. 'We all need to have allowances
made for us sometimes, don't we?'

After lunch and the hospital tour, Andie and Reba
returned to the charge nurse's office and Reba
explained routines and how the roster worked. Andie
was to work day shifts most of the time, doing a night
shift only when one of the part-time night nurses was
rostered off or there was an emergency. As theatre
work was not a full-time requirement, she was allo-
cated the women's wards for a start, which included
the birthing unit.

Reba told her, 'We don't have ops every day of the
week, and there are only occasional emergencies, but
we do have quite a lot of minor ops which don't
require the patient to be admitted. Splinters, cuts,
dislocations, burns, all that kind of thing, most of
which the GPs send up to us.' She looked at her watch,
then at Andie. 'You still look tired. Why don't you
run along home and settle yourself in, then have an
early night, and start properly tomorrow morning?'

'But I thought you said I'd be needed this
afternoon?'

'I did, but I didn't realise how drained you were.'

Reba regarded her new nurse with concern. 'Can't have you stressed this early in the piece! I'll scrub for Cam today. He can have one last chance to throw things at me! Go along, do as Sister tells you.'

Andie allowed herself to be persuaded. She was tired, and her fatigue was partly emotional, she knew. Running into Cam again had been a shock, and she was still feeling the effects, and still apprehensive about working with him. She was glad not to have to again today. She needed some time to think, to put it all into perspective.

Back in the annexe she made herself a cup of tea and then stretched out on the bed. She fell asleep almost at once, and it was gloomy in the room when she awoke. The sun was going down.

Feeling hungry, she went into the kitchen and contemplated her stores. 'Now, what shall I have for dinner?' she mused, taken aback at her extravagance.

The doorbell interrupted her decision-making. Not Cam, Andie thought, *please*. It wasn't. A motherly-looking woman in a floral print dress and apron stood on the step.

'I'm Jean,' she announced, 'Cam's housekeeper. Everything all right?' Her grey hair was tinted blue, and her eyes were warm.

'Oh—yes. Hello.' Andie held out her hand. 'Thank you for everything, Mrs Barlow.'

'Jean,' the woman insisted. 'And you're Andie. Is that short for something formidable?'

'Andrea.'

Jean nodded, and gave her an appraising look. 'Hmm. Andie suits you, though. It sounds tomboyish. Are you?'

Andie laughed. 'A bit, I suppose. I have three brothers, and I had to keep up with them or go under.'

'How lucky you are. I was an only child.'

Jean's manner was so warm and friendly, Andie

took to her at once. 'Would you like to come in?' she invited.

'No dear, thank you. I just popped over to see how you were making out. If there's anything you want, don't hesitate to come to the house and ask.'

'You live in?' Andie asked.

'Now I do. I used to come and do for Cam three days a week, but after my mother died last year—she was ninety and had been very frail for a long time—Cam suggested I rent my place and move in here. He's so kind. He saw at once that I was a bit lost.' Jean brushed away a tear. 'Mother wasn't the easiest of people to get on with, but I miss her nevertheless. You get out of the swim, too, looking after an old person, but Cam's good at urging me to have a social life again.

'We used to have the newsagency, you know, until my father had a stroke. Mum used to help up at the hospital, doing the flowers and other little jobs. I still do now and then. When Cam asked me to housekeep full-time and live in I jumped at it.' Jean laughed. 'Men! They all need someone to pick up after them and make sure they eat decent meals. And I must have something to do. Well, I mustn't stand here gossiping. I'll leave you to it, but, don't forget, anything you need, just ask.'

'Thanks, I will.' Andie was touched by Jean's considerateness.

Andie had eaten well at lunchtime, so she contented herself with a light salad and fruit meal, then set about hanging up her clothes and distributing her few personal belongings about.

She had just finished when there was another ring at the doorbell. Not Cam, please, she muttered. Again it wasn't, but her caller was not someone she particularly welcomed.

'Dr Lester. . .'

'Barry,' he said. 'I thought it was a bit mean to make

you wait till Saturday for a welcome, so I brought this
along. . .' he waved a bottle of champagne '. . .for a
little celebratory drink right now.'

Andie bit her lip. He looked so pleased with himself,
and the thought was nice, but. . . 'I was going to have
an early night,' she told him.

His face fell a fraction, but he quickly recovered.
'Not too early, I hope. It doesn't take long to knock
over a bottle of champers, and it'll make you sleep like
a log.' He smiled hopefully at her, and Andie hadn't
the will to be heartless.

'All right, come in,' she said. 'I've already eaten.
Have you?'

'Yes. My landlady would have fatal apoplexy if I
didn't turn up for dinner when I hadn't forewarned her
I'd be out. She glowers as though she doesn't believe
me even when I've been held up by an emergency.'

Andie laughed. She could see why Reba was smitten
with Barry. He did have a certain boyish charm. But
he wasn't the kind of man who could bowl her over.
She wasn't sure any man ever would again. Paul had
done it, and look what a mess that had turned out to
be. She wasn't going to put her heart in danger again.

'Not a bad little pad, this,' Barry commented as they
went through to the sitting-room. 'Nice and cosy.'

Andie said, 'I'll get some glasses.' She turned at the
door. 'Like some crackers?'

He nodded and began to untwist the wire on the
champagne cork. I mustn't encourage this sort of thing,
Andie told herself as she looked for glasses. I don't
want to make Reba jealous. She hurried back with the
glasses and a plate of Ritz crackers.

'Where do you hail from?' she asked the man
sprawled in one of the two armchairs.

'Kellerberrin.' He rose to pour the champagne.

Andie crooked an eyebrow. 'Where's that?'

'It's a wheatbelt town in Western Australia.'

She curled her fingers around the stem of the glass

he handed her. 'You're a long way from home,' she commented.

'Not as far as you are. What brought you to Australia and, more to the point, to Boobera?'

'Are you sure you want to hear? It's rather boring.' Andie looked him straight in the eye. At least the expurgated version was, and that was the only version he was going to hear.

Barry touched his glass to hers. 'Welcome to Boobera, Andie.'

'Thanks.'

'Now come and sit beside me and tell me all about yourself.' He glanced at the couch and moved towards it.

'You sound like a psychiatrist,' Andie said, and dropped into the armchair near her. She went on quickly, 'You go first. Tell me how you got from Kellerberrin to Boobera.'

By the time the champagne was finished, and there were only crumbs on the crackers plate, Andie had heard the story of Barry's life from childhood on a wheat farm as one of a large family, through medical school in Perth and then stints in general practice in various places throughout Australia.

'Evading fathers with shotguns!' he joked, but Andie wondered if there wasn't a grain of truth in it. He stopped smiling and looked at her sharply. 'Now tell me what you're evading—or rather whom?'

His unexpected perception threw her off balance, and she feared her face might have given her away.

'I haven't robbed any banks!' she said, a little too facetiously. She repeated her story of wanting a change, and when he asked about her family, she told him just the bare facts: how her parents had been killed in a train crash ten years before, and how her brothers had ensured that she was able to train as a nurse. She told him she'd always wanted to travel, but

that for the moment she intended to stay in Australia
and see as much of the country as she could.

'I can't believe there isn't a male somewhere in all
this,' he said finally. 'Besides brothers!'

'Would I tell you if there were?' she answered
archly, getting up. 'Would you like some coffee?'

He didn't say no. When they'd drunk it, Andie
yawned rather ostentatiously and said, 'Pardon me. . .'

Barry rose at once. 'OK, I can take a hint. You
want to go to bed.'

'I can't deny it.'

Ignoring his mockingly raised eyebrow, she moved
emphatically to the door and he followed. 'Thanks for
the champagne,' she said. 'It was a nice thought,
Barry, and I'm sure I shall sleep all the better for it.'

He looked at her for a moment as though considering something he might do or say which he then
thought the better of. 'I'll let you know about the party
on Saturday,' he said. 'Sleep tight, and don't work too
hard tomorrow. Edge yourself in slowly.'

'Goodnight, Barry, and thanks again,' she said,
holding the door open.

He said, 'Goodnight, Andie. See you,' and strode
off along the path. He was almost at the gate when a
car swung in off the road and headlights dazzled him,
and Andie too. She saw Barry in silhouette, raising his
arm to his face as he dodged to one side, then the
headlights disappeared and he walked on, only dimly
visible now in the glow from the distant street lamp.
Andie assumed that it was Cam who had driven in.
For some reason she wished he hadn't seen Barry.

'I thought you were going to start work *yesterday*.'
Cameron Walters's hard-edged voice brought Andie to
a quivering halt in the corridor, and she turned round.
His eyes were as chilly as ever. Yesterday's thaw must
have been her imagination.

'Reba said there was no need. I—I was very

tired. . .' Her long eyelashes flickered. He could still make her feel like some irresponsible flibbertigibbet.

His eyes roved slowly over her neat, uniformed figure, but with more censure than approval. 'You weren't too tired to entertain Dr Lester, though.' The words were quick, sharp and accusing.

Andie flushed guiltily, although she had no reason for guilt. That Cam could still make her feel that way angered her. She lifted her chin defiantly. 'Barry dropped by with a bottle of champagne to welcome me to Boobera. Anything wrong with that? I'd already had a rest by the time he arrived, and had my dinner.'

Cam looked grimly amused by her discomfort. 'Trust our Barry! He doesn't let the grass grow under his feet, but then neither do you, do you?'

Andie was incensed. 'What's that supposed to mean?' she demanded.

Cam shrugged. 'Just be sure you know what you're doing. Barry has quite a reputation in these parts, and he's apparently very popular with the ladies.'

'Jealous?' she could not resist gibing.

His brows dived together and the dark eyes narrowed, but all he said was, 'I'll be coming round the women's ward in about half an hour.' Unspoken was the command—'Be ready and all shipshape, or else!'

Andie gave him what she hoped was a disdainful look. 'We'll be waiting. . .' She was tempted to add 'with bated breath', but the look in his eyes told her that such daring might be going too far. She must not bring her personal dislike of the man to work. Here, he was professionally above her, and would have every right to reprimand her, as she had no doubt he would if she stepped over the line.

Gritting her teeth, she marched off into the larger of the two women's wards. It was just as well ward doors were swing doors, she thought, because she was in the mood for slamming one.

However, her chagrin evaporated quickly once she turned her attention to her patients. All the women were friendly, cheerful and appreciative, and the atmosphere in the ward was one of cameraderie. Unlike in a big city hospital, most of them knew each other, and their families. Andie noticed at once the difference in the conversation flying from bed to bed. In the city you didn't hear earnest discussion about the 'rural downturn', about droughts, livestock prices, and whether the school parents' committee could raise enough to replace the old school bus which was forever breaking down. Here, they were all involved with each other, and there was more mutual sympathy and understanding.

Two of the women were teasing a third whose locker was overflowing with flowers.

'Wait till you've been married as long as I have, Mandy,' laughed the grey-haired diabetic patient, Mrs Lomax. 'Then it'll be: "When are you going to come home? I'm out of clean shirts, and, the can-opener's broken down!"'

'She'll be lucky!' put in the woman in the bed on Mandy's other side. 'All I get is: "Can't do a thing with *your* kids, something's wrong with *your* stove, washing machine, iron, or lawnmower". As for flowers, I reckon even the geraniums'll be dead by the time I get home.'

'I don't think Warren will ever be like that,' said Mandy, half apologetically, half fearfully, Andie thought. 'He's so. . .so. . .sensitive.' She blushed, fluttering her eyelashes, and her mouth turned down a little as she swallowed hard. She was missing her husband, Andie thought, with sympathy. Just as she'd missed Paul, oh, so much, all those years ago when he'd gone home to Sydney without her. Maybe if she'd given up nursing and gone with him. . . She cut off the thought that had often plagued her. There was no time for self-recrimination now. Cam would be doing his rounds soon.

'Well, you'll soon be going home, Mandy,' she told the young woman. 'You'll be out of here before the flowers have wilted.' She wheeled her trolley closer and began to take her observations. 'How are you feeling?' she asked before popping a thermometer in the girl's mouth.

'I feel fine,' Mandy said. 'Really great.' But there was an underlying anxiety in her eyes, a faint quaver in her smile. Andie could guess why.

Mrs Amanda Lovett had been admitted with labour pains two days ago and had miscarried. It was only the fourth month, and she was probably worried, despite reassurances, that the miscarriage would affect her bearing a child in the future.

Andie bent close. 'Mandy, if there's anything worrying you, the slightest thing, you will talk to Dr Walters, won't you? It doesn't do any good to get yourself in a state over something that may not be a worry at all.'

Mandy smiled ruefully. She confessed in a whisper, 'I should hate to disappoint Warren. He does so love children.'

Andie gave her hand a squeeze. 'I'm sure you've got nothing to worry about. But you talk to Dr Walters. He'll be along shortly.'

Mandy seemed reluctant, and Andie was momentarily puzzled, then the penny dropped. She didn't want anyone to overhear her conversation. So Andie said in a low tone, 'It is a bit public, isn't it, even when the screens are around? If you'd rather, you can see him later, Mandy, in his office. I'll drop a word in his ear if you like.'

Mandy's expression eased. 'Would you? Thanks.' Her voice was almost inaudible as she whispered, 'They're very kind, but. . .'

Andie smiled. 'I know!'

She had spent rather longer chatting with Mandy

than she should have done, and any minute now, Cam would appear. She glanced across at Lenore who was busy tidying beds and lockers. Shipshape everything would be! And the examination trolley was all laid up ready and waiting in the corner. Dr Walters was not going to find any slovenliness here.

He came in just seconds after she had finished her obs and she hurried across to forestall him at the door before it become impossible to talk to him about Mandy. He paused as he entered because she was walking towards him, but he did not look at her. His eyes darted critically around the ward, and then finally came to rest on her as she halted in front of him.

'May I have a quick word?' she asked.

'Can't it wait?'

Andie recoiled from his brusqueness and stood her ground. 'No. It's about one of the patients. I want to speak to you before you see her.'

He turned back to the door. 'We'd better step outside, then.'

Andie was glad he'd said that. In the corridor she told him what Mandy had said. He nodded, but his eyes were intently on her face as though he wasn't listening.

'It's a very sensitive issue,' she explained, putting extra emphasis on her words because he didn't seem to be taking her very seriously. 'Men don't understand. . .'

Now he glowered at her. 'I have been a doctor for long enough to know when sensitivity is required. It's not impossible, you know, for a doctor to understand how a woman feels.'

'You never understood how *I* felt!' Andie heard herself saying, and clamped her teeth on her bottom lip in dismay. Her sudden upsurge of anger had caught her unawares.

Cam looked at her without responding, as though he wouldn't lower himself to. What had possessed her to stay? It was never going to work. If he was going to make her lash out at him like that, how could they work together? She gritted her teeth. She must learn to control herself better.

'After you,' Cam said, pushing the ward door open again.

CHAPTER FOUR

THE Saturday night party which Dr Lester had arranged to welcome Andie to Boobera was held in the school hall. Although she appreciated the gesture, at the last minute Andie wished he hadn't done it. She was not unsociable, but she did not particularly like being the centre of attraction or the butt of curiosity, no matter how friendly it was. When she said as much to Jean, Cam's housekeeper just laughed.

'Go on! You'll have a lovely time. You've got to let all the single males get a look at you. It's traditional!'

'You make it sound like a cattle market.'

Jean patted her shoulder. 'Well, it isn't. There are a few unattached fellows around here, but they're a pretty decent lot. Most are a bit reserved and very polite. They respect nurses more than anyone. They never know when they might need you!'

Andie pulled a face. 'Well, that'll make a change. A lot of people still see us as little better than skivvies.'

Jean said seriously, 'In Boobera, we've learned to value our medical staff, believe me. Your performance the day you arrived, and then getting old Mack into hospital so promptly, have made a pretty solid impression, I can tell you.'

Andie submitted with a smile. 'So, what shall I wear? What's traditional?'

'Wear one of your pretty cotton frocks.' Jean inclined her head, considering her for a moment. 'And wear your beautiful hair loose. A couple of pieces of jewellery wouldn't go amiss. We dress up a bit for parties in the hall.'

Andie chose a brown, orange and yellow print dress with a deep neckline and softly draped sleeves. The skirt was gathered into a wide belt at the waist and, although she wasn't aware of it, short enough to show off enough of her slender, shapely legs to make male heads turn. Taking Jean's advice, she wore her favourite gold chains and a filigree gold bracelet which she treasured because it had been her mother's.

The school was only two blocks away, so she walked there, savouring the cool night air which was perfumed with frangipani and the subtler scents of dry earth and grasses. As she walked down a dark side street, she was suddenly aware of the brightness of the myriad stars festooned above, and she stopped to gaze at them. It was so peaceful. When a car backfired and she smelled petrol fumes, it seemed like a wanton instrusion.

The hall was already full of people, but more were arriving as she walked up to the entrance. Andie was taken aback, and deeply touched, to find herself confronted by a large 'Welcome, Sister Andie' banner. She didn't have to introduce herself. Everyone knew who she was because she was the only stranger there. She found herself swept from one group to another, plied with drinks and nibbles, and endless questions. She was finally discovered by Barry.

'Sorry I wasn't here when you arrived.' He sounded breathless as he whispered in her ear. 'But better late than never. Which is what Louise Grant said about the bouncing baby boy I just delivered. Two weeks overdue, unless her calculations and mine were out.'

Andie shot him an anxious look. 'Was everything all right?' Mrs Grant had been admitted late that afternoon and she'd heard Reba muttering something about complications and a possible Caesarian.

'Right as rain. Master Grant just wasn't all that keen on making his entrance on to the world stage and was playing a little hard to get.'

'Did you have to do a Caesar?'

'No, I'm glad to say. I prefer to let nature take its

course as far as possible, and that is precisely what nature did this evening.'

'Labour couldn't have been long,' Andie observed.

'Much you know! Louise had been having a hell of a time for hours. They live way out on a cattle station and her husband was out mustering. The phone was on the blink, so she could only wait until he came back. She's a plucky kid. She was all set to deliver the baby by herself if need be.'

Andie was shocked. 'She should have come and stayed in the hospital once the baby was known to be overdue.'

Barry shrugged. 'I did advise her to do that, but when you've already got a couple of kids and a property to help run, you don't take a couple of weeks off unless you absolutely have to. People like the Grants can't afford to.'

'It sounds like nineteenth-century pioneering,' Andie said, appalled. 'Supposing her husband hadn't come home in time, supposing it had been a breech position, or the cord had been round its neck. . .?'

Barry reached out and ran his fingers through her softly waving hair, touching her nape. 'Let's talk about something else. I like to close the surgery door behind me when I leave at night.' He let his eyes rove over her face. 'You look quite spectacular with your hair down. You should do it more often.'

'What?' Andie had drifted momentarily, thinking of Louise Grant, miles from civilisation, about to have a baby, racked with labour pains and not knowing if she would make it to the hospital in time. She shuddered.

Barry's hand on her neck drew her closer. 'Let your hair down. . .' He removed the empty glass from her hand and placed it on a nearby table, then expertly guided her on to the dance-floor.

When it looked as though everyone who was coming had arrived, Barry dragged Andie to the microphone on the stage where the band was playing, and formally welcomed her, after which a six-year-old in a pink dress presented her with a huge bouquet of flowers. Andie was overcome, but she managed to say a few shaky words of thanks. Everyone clapped and called out 'welcome to Boobera' then Barry swept her off into another dance.

Andie found herself looking out for Cam, but she didn't really expect him to come. She resisted the temptation to ask Barry if he had invited him, because she didn't want to give any wrong impressions.

Most of the nurses and other staff from the hospital were there, except Reba, who had volunteered to do extra duty. Someone was going to relieve her later so she could have a couple of hours at the party, according to Jessica.

As the evening progressed, Andie met more and more people, became totally confused over names, and eventually began to develop a headache. But, since she was the guest of honour, she could scarcely excuse herself and go home. She did excuse herself once, however, to go outside for some fresh air to ease the ache behind her eyes.

When she stepped back into the hall, she was concealed behind people standing around the edge of the dance-floor, and looking between their shoulders, she suddenly started. Just across the room was Cam, looking around as though for someone. Her? Unexpectedly, her heart gave a curious little leap and she was about to go over to him when she halted. A stunning auburn-haired woman was gliding towards him, with open arms, and smiling into his eyes. Andie experienced a very peculiar sensation as she watched them kiss. If it had been anyone but Cam, she might have thought it was jealousy.

She dragged her eyes away and caught Barry's. He had spotted her and was weaving his way towards her. Andie pretended she had not seen Cam.

Barry draped an arm around her shoulders. 'Where have you been?' he asked.

'I went out for a breath of fresh air.'

He bent closer. 'Which has put roses back in your cheeks. You were looking a bit pale before.'

Andie clasped her hands over her cheeks and found them warm. She knew it wasn't the fresh air which had induced the colour, and was angry with herself.

Barry said, 'Oh-oh, there's Cam.' He didn't sound pleased.

Andie asked innocently, 'Cam? Did you ask him?'

'Of course I asked him. I asked everybody,' Barry said expansively.

'I thought he'd have gone to Marshall's Creek. Isn't that where he usually goes at weekends?' Andie felt an odd little surge of pleasure to think that Cam might have stayed in town just to go to her party.

Barry shattered her assumption. 'Yes, but he's on call this weekend. Didn't you know?'

Andie hadn't known. The confirmation that he hadn't stayed in town specifically to attend Barry's welcome party for her was sobering, but of course she'd been a fool to entertain such a possibility even for a minute. Still, he had come to the party. There was no need for him to have done that.

'But he had to come in specially last weekend,' she pointed out, thinking it was unfair.

Barry shrugged. 'I did offer, but he said it didn't matter. He'd only missed a bit of Sunday last week.'

'That was generous,' she commented. Cam hadn't sounded quite so generous at the time.

He nodded offhandedly. 'It wasn't my fault my beeper wasn't working.' He gave her an enigmatic look. 'Maybe he just wanted to come to your party!'

The band struck up a loud fanfare and the lights were dimmed as the introductory racket faded into a dreamier tempo. When a hand descended on to Andie's shoulder, she turned quickly, and saw Cam looking down at her, not quite smiling, but pleasant enough. The glamorous woman was no longer with him.

He glanced at Barry. 'You can spare Andie for a dance, I'm sure.'

'Go for it!' said Barry goodhumouredly. 'If the lady's willing, I am! We haven't got tickets on each other yet, as my old granny used to say!'

Cam did not smile. He wasn't the kind of man to appreciate facetiousness, Andie thought. She recalled vividly his angry reaction when Paul, who was inclined not to take his older brother seriously, had taken refuge in levity. Cam's tongue-lashing had quietened even the irrepressible Paul. She remembered being frightened of Cam's anger, yet also fascinated in a strange, compulsive kind of way. Those dark eyes burning like hot coals, slightly flaring nostrils, and full firm lips castigating his brother with words she could not afterwards recall, had been astonishingly sensuous, causing a churning sensation in the pit of her stomach that conflicted with the way she really felt about him.

Looking at him now, Andie felt an echo of her feelings on that far-off occasion, and was alarmed. But Cam had already slid an arm around her and was guiding her on to the dance-floor. He clasped her hand and held her close. His preference was obviously for the more old-fashioned kind of dancing.

Andie inclined her head towards a group of other dancers who were all energetically gyrating separately.

'Don't you like the modern way?' she asked, with a teasing look up into his face.

Cam bent his head slightly and his dark eyes held hers for a moment. 'We can dance that way if you want?'

Why his tone made it difficult for her to say yes, she did want, she wasn't sure. She didn't want him to think she was provocative, so she replied, 'Not especially. This is fine.'

But was it? Dancing with Cam was a strange experience. Being held in his arms was more disturbing than she'd expected. She had never imagined herself in Cam Walters's arms, dancing. . .or. . . Unbidden, a bizarre fantasy invaded her thoughts—Cam kissing her—and she felt a prickling warmth steal over her. Was she out of her mind?

They circled the dance-floor two or three times, not talking much, and when they did the conversation was on medical topics. Andie did not feel at ease with him, but there was a curious kind of pleasure in gliding around the floor to the rhythm of moody music in Cam's arms.

Barry was not dancing, and each time they passed him, he raised his glass slightly and smiled at Andie. The third time round, Cam stopped suddenly and let her go. It was a moment before she realised why, because her back had been towards Barry. Now she saw that he had company, the auburn-haired woman.

The woman held out her hand to Andie. 'You must be the guest of honour. I'm Madeleine Trentham.'

Andie felt as though she was suddenly standing in shadow. 'How do you do?' she said, noting the wary look in the other woman's eyes.

'Welcome to Boobera,' said Madeleine, looking Andie over rather more subtly than most people had. 'I hope you've settled in all right.'

'Yes, thank you. Everyone has been very kind.' Andie felt gauche. Madeleine Trentham was no unsophisticated country girl, although she certainly wasn't overdressed for the occasion. Her blue and white glazed cotton trousers and top were casual enough, but Andie suspected that, whatever clothes she wore, Madeleine would always look elegant. It was hardly surprising that Cam wanted to marry her.

'Country people are like that,' said Madeleine, with slight disdain.

Andie's reaction to Madeleine was not to take an

instant dislike to her, but to regard her with the same reservations as she was sure Cam's companion was feeling towards her.

Cam said, 'Shall we sit down?'

'There's a free table.' Barry made a beeline for it, and when the others joined him he offered, 'Drinks, everyone?'

He and Cam went off to fetch them, and Madeleine made polite conversation, asking Andie where she came from and why she had chosen to work in outback South Australia. Andie gave her stock replies, but, unlike most other people, she seemed not altogether convinced by Andie's explanation.

A sceptical smile curved her wide mouth. 'Most people who come up here are escaping from someone or something,' she said. 'Usually a broken romance. . .' An invitation to confess hung in the air.

Andie wondered if Cam had told her about Paul and his brother's ill-fated marriage to the English girl he had disapproved of. She said, 'Well, that wasn't the reason I came here.'

'No?' Madeleine raised one finely arched eyebrow. 'Well, if you say so, dear.' She went on, 'You're staying in the annexe, I gather?'

'Yes.'

Madeleine laughed. 'And Jean's doing her best to mother you, I bet.' She leaned slightly across the table. 'You don't look to me like someone who needs mothering!' Her faintly arch tone was tempered by a quick smile.

Andie said, 'Oh, we're all vulnerable sometimes, I suppose.'

Madeleine leaned back in her chair, legs crossed elegantly. Her shirt was open low enough to reveal the curve of a full bosom, and her skin was smooth and lightly tanned. 'To men especially,' she murmured. She tapped two perfectly manicured fingertips on the table. 'Just a kindly word of warning, Andie—Barry

trifles with the affections of the women who fall for
him.'

'Like Reba?' Andie hadn't meant to gossip, the
remark had just slipped out.

Madeleine nodded. 'Like poor Reba. She's besotted
with the man, and he takes advantage of her all the
time.' She paused, smiling. 'He throws a welcome
party for all the new nurses, you know.'

'Maybe he's just a good-hearted chap,' Andie said,
feeling she had been deliberately cut down to size.

'He likes to be the first one to get his foot in the
door! Now Cam is quite different. Cam is a wonderful
guy and I'm so lucky to have met him. I was very
lonely after my husband died, totally bereft, and Cam
helped me to get back on my feet again. I owe him
such a lot.'

'Yes, Jean said he'd helped her wonderfully after
her mother died,' Andie said, then realised from
Madeleine's frown that she had unwittingly turned the
tables. She smiled to show that no sarcasm had been
intended and went on, 'It's part of a doctor's vocation
to comfort. . .' Seeing that her words weren't repairing
the damage, she broke off, just as the two men
returned with their drinks.

Andie realised then that Madeleine had not really
been warning her about Barry, but warning her off
Cam. She had no need to worry, she thought wryly.
She remarked, 'Reba said your property is a tourist
resort.'

Madeleine accepted her drink from Cam, her fingers
touching his, her eyes lifted to his with an intimate
look. 'Thank you, darling.' She turned back to Andie
with a façade of friendliness. 'Yes. It was long past its
prime as a cattle station and more of a financial drain
than an asset when Hugo bought the place. It was his
idea to turn it into a tourist attraction, and I must say
it's been very successful. We still keep a few head of
cattle, of course, for atmosphere, and people can come

and stay and see how a cattle station works, take part
in mustering and see all those cruel things. . .' she
pulled a distasteful face '. . .like de-horning and
branding.'

'All very necessary,' said Barry, 'if you're going to
have steaks for dinner.'

Madeleine reminded him sweetly, '*I* don't.' She
glanced up at Cam again. 'I wish Hugo had turned the
place into a wildlife sanctuary like Marshall's Creek,
but of course that wasn't practicable. We weren't rich
like Cam! We had to have an income. But I shall sell
the place as soon as I can find a buyer. An old friend
of Hugo's is interested, so I'm keeping my fingers
crossed.'

'You'll go back to the city?' Barry asked. He
explained briefly to Andie, 'Madeleine used to manage
a fashionable boutique in Sydney.'

Madeleine's mouth seemed to be repressing a smile,
and her answer was cryptic. 'That all depends, Barry,'
she said, and her eyes were on Cam's face, not the
younger doctor's.

The music had started up again, a lively rhythm
which made Barry tap one foot on the table leg. He
held out his hand to Andie. 'Come on.'

Andie let herself be whisked away into the swelling
crowd of dancers moving back on to the floor. As
before, Barry danced apart from Andie, and he was
very good. Catching his energetic rhythm, Andie
enjoyed herself, but when he finally gathered her into
his arms and whirled her off tightly clasped against his
chest, she felt a sense of deprivation and didn't know
why. When they passed the table where they had been
sitting, Cam and Madeleine were talking earnestly.

Barry murmured in her ear, 'I know why Cam was
so keen to keep to the roster. Madeleine had to come
to Boobera for the weekend to fix up new arrange-
ments for her tourists who want to stop over at the
hotel.'

Andie laughed. 'How do you know that?'

He grinned back at her. 'You can't blink in Boobera without everyone knowing and speculating!'

'So it seems.' Andie caught herself wishing Cam would be called out to an emergency.

As though her wish had been granted, the next time round he had gone, but so had Madeleine. Andie didn't believe Cam had been called to the hospital. She felt a curious ache under her ribs. Where were they? A moment later she saw them, dancing, closely entwined as she and Cam had been earlier, and Madeleine was laughing up into his face while he smiled down at her. Lovers? Andie wondered. Yes, of course they are, she told herself, and was shocked because she minded. Unthinkingly, she rested her head wearily against Barry's shoulder, wishing her emotions were not in such a turmoil. He, of course, took her gesture completely the wrong way.

His lips brushed her forehead and he held her closer as he murmured, 'I hope you're going to let me take you home tonight.'

Andie pulled herself together and raised her head. 'It's only two blocks. I walked.'

'Anything can happen in two blocks.'

'In Boobera?' she teased.

He gave her a mock-sombre look. 'It's my duty to protect our valuable nursing staff.'

Andie did not want him to take her home, since she was afraid it might be difficult to get rid of him if she did, but she couldn't be rude. After all, Barry had gone to a lot of trouble to organise this party for her. If he got fresh, she would just have to be firm, she decided.

As the evening progressed, she danced most of the time, with Barry and several other men, but not with Cam again. He seemed glued to Madeleine's side. It was after supper, and Andie was dancing with Barry, when Cam suddenly appeared, alone, and beckoned them to the edge of the dance-floor. His face was grim, and Andie sensed instantly that something was wrong.

'Got to go. Sorry,' he said to Barry. 'Urgent appendicectomy.'

Barry groaned. 'The perennial party-pooper. Want any help?' he offered.

'I can manage,' Cam said briskly. 'But if Andie wouldn't mind coming along. . .' He looked questioningly at her.

'Hey, wait, it's her party!' protested Barry, taking Andie's arm in a restraining grip.

'I know—I'm sorry,' Cam said, 'but it sounds as though it might be a tricky one. The patient's had attacks of acute appendicitis before, and Ralph suspects perforation and the possibility of an abscess.'

'Hell. I'd better come with you,' Barry said reluctantly, with a glance at Andie.

'There's no need for you to,' Cam insisted quite firmly. 'Ralph's there. He can handle the anaesthetic.'

Barry looked annoyed now. 'It's a shame to take Andie away,' he complained. 'Surely Reba can cope?'

'It seems unnecessary to expect her to when a more experienced theatre nurse is available,' Cam said. He looked at Andie. 'You don't *have* to come.'

'Of course I'll come.' Andie wouldn't have dreamed of refusing, and, besides, it was her chance to avoid being taken home by Barry. 'The party won't go on much longer, anyway, will it?' She had wondered why Reba hadn't yet put in an appearance.

Cam gave her a thin smile. 'Right, let's go, then. Look after Madeleine, Barry, and make apologies where necessary.'

In the Range Rover it was only a couple of minutes to the hospital. He wouldn't dare drive like that in city traffic, Andie reflected. Stones flew up from the wheels and the brakes squealed as he cornered tightly.

Dr Ralph Warrington was waiting for them. He seldom operated now, Cam had told her in the car. He was seventy and still a first-class GP, but he had decided of his own accord to give up theatre work. All he was prepared to do was act as anaesthetist when necessary.

'Where the hell have you been?' he greeted them brusquely.

Andie had heard of his reputation for abrasiveness, but so far she had not encountered him.

'Coming,' said Cam calmly. 'This is Sister Somers. Andie, Dr Warrington.'

The elderly doctor glowered at her and muttered something she did not catch. It sounded more like a grumble than a greeting.

'How's the patient?' Cam asked.

'You'd better see for yourself.'

Andie went to scrub up and Reba joined her briefly. 'Oh, good, I'm glad he brought you. Doc Warrington's driving me crazy as usual. I'd be bound to drop something if I had to do it. That man makes me so nervous!'

But it's Cam who makes me nervous, Andie thought.

Reba helped her with her gown and cap. 'I've laid up the instruments, Andie. It's all ready to go.'

'Is the patient male or female?' Andie asked.

'Male—young bloke, plays a lot of football. Some say that strenuous exercise like that could be a contributing factor to appendicitis in young men. His mum says it's all the junk food he eats!'

'How critical is he?'

'Doc Warrington's worried, but he does tend to panic a bit these days. Cam'll know as soon as he goes in.'

'Andie!'

Cam's voice carried to them, and they hurried to do his bidding. Another nurse, a part-timer who did night shifts and whom Andie had only met once, was already in the theatre. Dr Warrington was hovering, his brow deeply creased above his mask. He was administering the anaesthetic. Andie and Reba prepared the operation site and arranged the sterile drapes.

'He takes it as a personal failure if one of his patients dies,' Reba whispered. 'One of these days he'll have a heart attack with worrying.' She raised her eyes briefly to the ceiling. 'But please, not tonight!'

Cam consulted with Dr Warrington and moments later the operation began. Cam exchanged a brief look with Andie as she handed him the skin knife. Soon they would know how serious the young man's condition was. As had been the case on the previous occasions she had worked with him, her concentration on the job in hand overrode all personal conflict and Cam became just a surgeon doing a job and she a nurse assisting him. It was just as well, she thought. The close working relationship needed between doctor and nurse in such circumstances would have been impossible otherwise.

She handed him retractors and mounted swabs expertly and quickly so Cam never had to ask twice. Until one unguarded moment when she caught his eye and dropped a swab on the floor.

She heard his muffled and impatient expletive as she hastily rolled another, and was chagrined by her tiny lapse of efficiency.

Then she heard Cam speak in a different tone. 'Bloody hell!'

Out of the corner of her eye, Andie saw Dr Warrington, by the patient's head, jerk forward, peering, but he was too far from the operation site to see properly.

'What is it?' he demanded.

Cam's face was tense, but his fingers were supple. 'As you suspected, Ralph, an abcess. Not pretty.'

Andie anticipated what that meant. Cam would open and drain the abcess, but probably not remove the appendix itself while the area was so inflamed and there was a danger of peritonitis.

'I told him to have it out twelve months ago,' Dr Warrington complained, his voice muffled by the mask, his tone indignant.

'Can't tell these young folk anything,' said Cam, and caught Andie's eye again.

She looked quickly away, not sure if he was making a personal point or not.

'Well, he'll be missing a few more football matches than he might have done,' said Dr Warrington, not without some grim satisfaction.

It was well after midnight when the operation was finished, the patient dosed with antibiotics, and returned with a drain in place to the care of the night nurse. Reba had stayed on and looked weary.

'I think I'll have to give your party a miss,' she said. 'Are you going back?'

Andie felt rather tired herself. She shook her head. 'It'll be breaking up now, surely?' Besides, home and a soft bed seemed much too attractive an alternative.

'Want me to give you a lift?' Reba offered.

Andie thanked her. She was walking down the corridor, about to leave, when Cam's voice halted her.

'Where are you going?'

She turned. He was still in theatre greens, mask dangling around his neck, cap pushed back so that his dark hair was flopping over his forehead in that curiously boyish fashion it sometimes did.

'Home. You don't want me any more now, do you?'

He came up to her. 'No. But I'll be going myself shortly. You can't walk all the way home at this hour. Don't be ridiculous.'

'Reba's offered me a lift,' she told him.

'Seeing we live on the same premises, there's no need to take her out of her way.'

'I thought you might not be ready to go yet.'

He dropped a hand on her shoulder. 'I am. Everything's under control here. Even Ralph's gone home!'

Andie smiled. 'He is a worrier, isn't he?'

Cam nodded. 'It used to be conscientiousness. Nowadays it's just that he's not so sure of himself.' He looked steadily at her. 'Sorry you were dragged from your party.'

'I didn't mind. It was nearly over anyway.'

'Thanks, nevertheless.'

He dropped a hand on her shoulder for emphasis and left it there. For a moment, in the dimly lit corridor, they faced each other in uneasy silence, as though each wanted to say something vital, but as though neither had the courage, or the temerity, to do so. Then Cam let his hand fall to his side, and said, 'Let's get going. You can help me out of this gear first.'

Reba reappeared, ready to go, and Cam said, 'It's OK, Reba, I'll take Andie home.'

Andie walked back to the gowning-room with him and untied the tapes of his theatre gown. When the discarded clothing was disposed of and Cam had donned his shirt and jacket, they left.

As they walked to the Range Rover, Andie took a deep breath of cool night air to clear the antiseptic smells from her lungs. She felt a surge of elation, the kind of high that came sometimes when you knew a job had been well done. It wasn't as though the operation had been difficult or even dangerous, although there had been cause for concern and still was to an extent, it was more a feeling of relief.

'I suppose Barry was hoping to escort you home tonight,' Cam remarked, as they turned out of the hospital gates.

'He did suggest it was part of his duty to protect the nursing staff,' Andie answered.

He laughed. 'He would!'

'You don't mind that he took Madeleine back to the hotel instead?' she asked.

Cam slid a half-smiling glance at her. 'Madeleine? She can take care of herself.'

Andie bridled a bit. 'So can I!'

Cam didn't reply. They were already at the house and he turned smoothly into the driveway. As the headlights swept across her car, Andie asked, 'Is my car OK there?'

He braked sharply and gravel flew. 'Perfectly,' he said.

She got out and he came round to her side. 'I'd better be as protective as Barry and see you right to your door,' he said. 'Who knows what might be lurking in the shrubbery?'

'Don't be ridiculous!'

'I was thinking maybe Barry. . .'

His mocking tone made Andie flare. 'There's no need to be insulting!'

He caught hold of her elbow and urged her along the pathway to the annexe. She did not protest. She didn't even care that he had been making fun of her. At the porch, she edged away from him.

'Thanks,' she said crisply. 'Goodnight, Cam.'

He had one hand on the porch post and was looking down at her. 'Goodnight, Andie,' he murmured, and leaned forward to kiss her forehead. 'Sorry I spoiled your party, but thanks.'

Andie was so astonished that she jerked back and momentarily lost her footing. Cam's effort to steady her meant that she ended up in his arms, with his mouth covering hers as he kissed her fiercely. The shock she suffered was not so much because he had kissed her, but because her body was responding to the act in an extraordinary and alarming way. This was a man she had come close to hating, a man who, she knew, despised her, and yet he was turning her emotions inside out. What was more, he seemed to be enjoying it as much as she was trying not to.

At last he stopped, and, lips still parted, looked hard

at her, almost as though seeing her for the first time. Andie was too shocked to speak. She was trembling on the brink of irrational tears.

'Now I know what Paul saw in you,' Cam said calmly, not a trace of emotional tremor in his voice. 'You know how to stir a man up, Andrea. But it doesn't last, does it? You soon tire and want someone new.'

Andie was shocked and bewildered by his words. '*I* do? You can't mean that, Cam. I wasn't the fickle one. It was Paul who left me, remember?'

He looked at her with growing distaste. 'There's no point in lying to me, Andie. Paul was distraught when you left him. Inconsolable, in fact.'

'Rubbish!' Andie was angry now. 'Paul had already been unfaithful to me before I arrived in Sydney. It was Paul who liked variety, who tired of relationships and wanted new ones, and no doubt still does.' Suddenly all the hurt and humiliation was welling up, and his accusation was a deep wound that no sutures could heal. She could tell, even in the dim light of the porch lamp, that he didn't believe her.

Shattered, she whispered incredulously, 'You don't believe me. . .'

'Of course I don't,' Cam said bluntly. 'Why should I believe you? We both know you're lying.'

'I am not lying!' Andie felt her control reach breaking point. 'You must know Paul walked out on me, that he was going to marry the girl he'd got pregnant, only he didn't because she lost the baby.'

Cam's face muscles tightened. 'All I know is that he came to me in great distress because you'd walked out on him. He said you'd left him for another man. He realised at last that I'd been right, that the marriage was a mistake, and that he'd allowed you to persuade him into it.'

'I never persuaded him! He didn't need any persuasion. He. . .he. . .'

'Thought he was in love with you,' finished Cam
icily. 'I'm not so sure that you were ever in love with
him, though. It was just a big adventure, wasn't it?
Getting married, going to Australia; and you didn't
believe any more than he did that I'd continue to stand
in the way of his inheriting his share of our grandfather's estate. You thought his needing my approval
to marry was ridiculous. You persuaded him to defy
me, and thought you could soften me up, didn't you?
When you found you were wrong, you got out at the
first opportunity.'

Andie felt as though the sky was crashing in on her.
'This is slander, lies! I never persuaded him to defy
you. And it was Paul who left me.' Her voice was
hoarse, almost a whisper, not very convincing.

'That's not what he told me.'

'And you believe him rather than me.' Andie felt
defeated.

'He is my brother. I saw how upset he was. I could
have killed you for doing that to him, for proving that
my judgement was right. If only he'd listened to
me. . .'

Andy clung to the porch railing. 'I don't think there's
any point in discussing it any more,' she said, adding
bitterly, 'I knew I should have left that first day. I was
crazy to stay.'

'Why did you?' he asked.

Andie forced herself to look at him fully. 'Because
you called me a coward, and I'm not a coward. And I
also stayed because of Reba and. . .' She trailed away.
She couldn't tell him that she'd stayed because she also
wanted to make peace between them. Now she knew
there was no chance she ever would. Paul had lied,
and there was no way she would ever be able to
convince Cam of that, or to make Paul tell the truth.

Cam said, 'You can't go now. Not when you've just
had a welcome party. As I said before, our past
association shouldn't be a factor in your being here.'

He looked long and hard at her. 'I might have forgiven you, if you'd just told the truth.'

'I am telling the truth,' Andie whimpered desperately.

Cam's expression did not soften. 'Perhaps it's just as well to have brought it out in the open,' he said. 'And now let's forget the whole thing. Goodnight, Andie.'

He turned and left her standing there, her knuckles gripping the railing until they were white, her whole body trembling with anger, frustration, and sheer misery. She watched his shadow disappear among the shrubs and trees near the house, and silently she vowed, 'No, I won't go, Cam. Somehow I'll make you believe me, somehow. . .'

CHAPTER FIVE

DR CAMERON WALTERS had never felt quite so shaken by any encounter with a woman as he did over his quarrel with Andrea Somers. It left him drained and feeling shabby somehow.

What in heaven's name had possessed him to kiss her? He pulled on his pyjama bottoms and knotted the cord, before flinging himself down on his bed. It was warm enough not to need bedclothes, or a top. He lay with his arms folded behind his head, staring at the darkness over his head. All right, she was an attractive woman, and when the tension eased, as it always did after an operation, other emotions could sometimes make a man vulnerable.

But the nerve of her! To try and pretend that Paul was the one at fault, that she was the injured party. . . It took his breath away.

Cam tossed restlessly, sudden uneasiness plaguing the back of his mind. What if she hadn't been lying? What if Paul had. . .?

He wiped a hand across his forehead, which was damp. If only the pair of them had been prepared to wait a few months—but they hadn't. They'd wanted to get married right away, even though they'd only known each other a few weeks. Paul had been twenty-one, Andie twenty. Just kids. Of course, Paul had been anxious to get his hands on his share of their grandfather's money, which he could only do before he was thirty if he married someone Cam approved of. That rankled, of course, because it underlined the fact that Grandfather had not had as high an opinion of Paul's good sense as Cam's. 'That lad needs a good woman to settle him down,' Jake Walters had said, and he had charged Cam with making sure that Paul wasn't seduced by 'some greedy little gold-digger'. Cam hadn't wanted that responsibility, but as he had looked after his younger brother after the car crash which had killed their parents when Paul was ten, he had accepted it. He had always been protective of Paul—perhaps over-protective, he now thought.

He remembered with some pain the confrontations with his brother, and with Andie, in London. He had grudgingly admired her spirit then, the way she had stuck up for Paul, but he had been afraid of her youth, afraid that the prospect of a considerable inheritance might be influencing her. And he'd also been afraid that Paul had merely fallen in love with her because she was beautiful.

He'd said some harsh things then which he regretted now, and it hadn't done any good. They had married. He couldn't prevent them doing that, but he had stood firm and refused to approve of the marriage. He had intended to give it a year or two to see if marriage would hasten their maturity, and then, if all was well, recommend to the trustees that Paul be paid his legacy.

But his worst fears had been realised. Within eighteen months, Andie had left Paul—for someone richer than he was, Paul had said bitterly. If Cam hadn't opposed the marriage and denied him his inheritance, he'd raged, everything would have been all right. Paul was rarely in touch now; there had been too much bitterness, and they were estranged. Cam worried because he knew Paul tended to drift from job to job or one hare-brained enterprise to the next. Maybe if he hadn't disapproved of Paul's marriage to Andie. . .

Cam sat bolt upright, burying his face in his hands. Feeling guilty about it now was pointless. Maybe he shouldn't have been so harsh, maybe he should have approved of them marrying, but at the time he couldn't. It hadn't just been their youth and his distrust of Andie's motives; he'd had a deep gut feeling that they were wrong for each other. And the strange thing was, it hadn't just been Paul he'd been concerned about, it had been Andie too. He hadn't wanted her to suffer disappointment and unhappiness.

Cam switched on a light and floundered out to the kitchen. He took a can of beer from the fridge, flipped off the ring top and drank it down in almost one gulp. What was he going to do? He'd made a big mistake tonight, first kissing the girl, then attacking her. It was she who had said it would be embarrassing for them to work together, and now he'd made it much worse.

'That's a nasty gash, Mr Thompson,' Andie said, as she finished cleaning the wound in the patient's thigh. The edges were ragged, but it had not bled over-much. Luckily the blade had missed the femoral artery. 'You're going to need quite a few stitches, I'm afraid.' He was a council worker who had been pruning street trees when his power saw had slipped.

He gave her a stoical grin. 'At least I didn't hack me leg right off!'

'And it was lucky you were wearing long trousers,' Andie reminded him. 'It might have been worse if you'd been wearing shorts like most of the men seem to around here. The cloth wasn't much protection, but it was something.'

Dean Thompson was the only patient in the casualty room, and Andie was waiting for Cam to come and look at him. She was confident that he would attend to the wound right there, and not want the patient moved to the theatre. A local anaesthetic would be all that was needed, she judged.

The door flew open and Cam walked in. 'G'day, Dean,' he said cheerily. 'Been trying to prune yourself as well as the trees again?'

Andie laughed as she disposed of the bloodstained swabs in the bin. 'Oh, he does it regularly, does he?'

Cam came over to the table. 'What was the problem

this time, Dean? Head in the clouds over some wench, or a hangover?' He looked straight at Andie as he spoke, and her pulse quickened as she remembered their angry confrontation on Saturday night. There was no acrimony in his eyes now, but no apology either.

'Get out!' scoffed the patient. 'I was just doin' me job, that's all. The ladder moved a bit, and I tried to save meself and—well, there you are.'

'And here *you* are!' Cam pulled on the sterile surgical gloves Andie held out to him and examined the leg. 'One limb less on a tree doesn't matter,' he said gravely, 'but you can't afford to lose one, Dean. You'd better take more care. This is your third accident in the last few months.'

'I know.' The man looked worried. 'You don't reckon they'll sack me, do you?'

'Not while you've still got both arms and legs,' joked Cam.

'Am I going to be laid up for long?'

'That'll depend on how this heals. Mmm, it's a deep wound, and there's some damage to the muscle. Now, hold tight while Sister Somers and I stitch you up.' He looked up at Andie, who interpreted his unspoken requirement, moving the intrument trolley to within closer reach.

'Novocaine?' she asked, breaking open a sterile hypodermic package.

Cam nodded. His hand was already reaching impatiently for the syringe before she'd even measured the anaesthetic drug into it. Andie finished the task without haste and put the syringe into his hand.

'This won't hurt,' Cam promised as he slid the needle under the skin to deaden the area around the gaping wound. He chatted cheerfully to the man on the table while they waited for the anesthetic to take effect and Andie prepeared needles and sutures.

She watched intently as Cam drew the two edges of the wound together, ensuring that they met in as good apposition as possible, without any folding under of the tissue, which might delay healing and make the injury more liable to infection. Her eyes followed his strong, supple fingers as they passed the needle through the skin at right angles to ensure the precise alignment, making a neat row of stitches—that would make an embroiderer proud, she thought. Dean would have minimum scar tissue.

As she snipped the last one for him, Cam said, 'We'll use a spray-on dressing, then we can keep an eye on the wound without disturbing it.'

Andie had anticipated this need, and a faint smile crossed his lips when she instantly provided the plastic spray.

'You've kept up your tetanus jabs, I hope, Dean,' Cam said, as he finished off the procedure to the wounded leg.

'Yes. Council insists.'

'Good. We'll give you a booster and an antibiotic and that should do the trick. I want you to stay in for a couple of days, and then keep off your leg for a week or so, at least until the stitches come out.'

'Right-oh,' Dean agreed resignedly.

'You can move him into the ward now,' Cam told Andie.

'Can I have a shower?' asked Dean. 'I feel a bit grubby and sweaty.'

Cam advised Andie, 'Best give him a bed-bath now, but he can have a proper one tomorrow, so long as he doesn't put too much pressure on that leg. No standing in the shower for a couple of days, Dean—I don't want that wound opening up.'

Andie nodded, and wheeled the trolley towards the door. 'I'll get a bed trolley and another nurse to help.'

'I'll give you a hand,' Cam offered amiably, holding the door open and following her out.

She glanced at him in surprise. She wouldn't have got that sort of offer from a physician or surgeon in a city hospital. But this was Boobera, in outback South Australia, and the hospital didn't have orderlies and theatre technicians to do such chores. Everyone helped.

'Thanks,' she said.

Cam strolled along the corridor with her to fetch the trolley, saying, 'Dean Thompson is diabetic, so I want a specially careful eye kept on that wound. You know diabetics have problems with slow tissue healing?'

'Of course.'

'There's always a chance of gangrene too. Or ulcers.'

Andie paused outside the medications room, and Cam opened the door so she could push the instrument trolley inside. She looked at him thoughtfully.

'If he's become accident-prone, could it be something to do with being diabetic? If he's not balancing his sugar and insulin properly, he could be getting the shakes, couldn't he?' Another thought occurred to her. 'Does he drink? You said something about a hangover, or were you joking?'

Cam studied her face. She could look so earnest sometimes that it almost brought tears to his eyes. This woman he knew as a highly competent nurse whose dedication was never in question, this woman with intelligence and compassion, was certainly a far cry from the impetuous girl his brother had married. Or the girl he'd thought she was. Perhaps he had not looked far enough beneath the surface then. He curbed his thoughts. The fact remained, she had lied to him. . .

'He does drink,' he told her. 'He's been warned about it, of course, but what can you do in a town like this where having a few beers with your mates at the pub after work is standard behaviour? You can't deprive a man of that. You could be right, though. It might be medication rather than alcohol causing him to be light-headed in the mornings. We'll do a thorough check. Take four-hourly observations from now, and we'll do a blood-test in the morning before he has any food. He might need stabilising and then a change of dosage.'

'How old is he? Fifty?' she asked.

'Forty-two. We age faster up here—it's the heat.'

Cam hadn't aged much, Andie thought. He looked very little different physically from when she had met him five years ago, but of course he was nowhere near forty yet. Thirty-five maybe. He would be more careful, though, than men like Dean Thompson. Cam didn't drink to excess, she was sure, and he didn't have to work out of doors. It was obvious that he also kept himself fit, and there wasn't a trace of grey in the dark hair, not even at the temples.

There was a sudden silence, with both of them standing in the corridor as though they'd forgotten what it was they had to do. For one ghastly moment Andie thought he was going to mention Saturday night, but he didn't. Like her, it seemed he was trying to forget what had happened, both the kiss and the quarrel. That was all they could do, she thought. Just forget it. But one day, she would make him believe. . .

'Better get poor old Dean made comfortable,' said Cam, breaking the spell. He ran his fingers through the unruly waves that tumbled over his forehead, ineffectually brushing them back.

The patient was swiftly transferred to the ward, where Marion Gore was in charge, and Andie went back to the medications room to unload her trolley and sterilise the instruments. Then it was back to the women's ward for an hour or so before lunch. The pace was not hectic, but she wasn't sure whether she appreciated that or not. It gave her rather too much time to think—about Cam, and Paul, and how things might have been. And yet she could not regret that her marriage to Paul had ended. It wasn't just his infidelity. There had been a basic incompatibility; she knew that now. She had been bowled over by Paul's charm and self-confidence, his romantic wooing of her, his adventurous streak, and she had failed to see his weaknesses, his tendency to exaggerate, his failure to face reality, his petulance when he didn't get his own way, and his deceit. There was a flaw in Paul, an innate irresponsibility and selfishness. But could you blame people for being born what they were? Andie sighed over it.

During the following fortnight Andie saw very little of Cam. Whether it was coincidental or whether he was deliberately cutting their contact to a minimum she couldn't tell, but instead of feeling grateful she felt depressed. It was hateful having him believe she was the guilty party, and even more hateful knowing he believed her to be a liar. She told herself over and over that it didn't matter a damn what he thought, but deep down she admitted that it did. It was similar to how she'd felt five years ago, she realised. She had hated him most because he had thought her unworthy of his brother, and subconsciously she had wanted to rate high in his estimation. She had, she realised uneasily, admired the man even then, even when he was bitterly opposed to her.

As the days went by, Andie gradually became absorbed in the social life of Boobera; Barry saw to that. Knowing Reba's feelings about Barry made Andie feel a little embarrassed about his attentions, but Reba was never anything but friendly and kind. She seemed resigned to the fact that Dr Lester was a man who liked playing the field.

Reba said rather wistfully one day, when she and Andie were having a cup of tea together in the quiet of the charge nurse's office, 'Are you sleeping with Barry?'

Andie was startled by her directness and coloured involuntarily. 'No! What made you think. . .?' She broke off. It was an obvious conclusion, she supposed.

Reba stirred her tea desultorily. 'It doesn't matter if you are. I know Barry. I know I couldn't keep him even if I did sleep with him.'

'Well, I'm not,' Andie said. 'I'm not attracted to him that way.'

'If I know Barry, he hopes you will be eventually.' Reba smiled faintly. 'He's very confident of his charm.'

Andie saw the hurt in the other nurse's eyes, and felt guilty again. 'Maybe one of these days he will decide to settle down,' she said.

A shadow of anger crossed Reba's face. 'Well, he needn't think I'll still be hanging around when he does!'

Andie suppressed a smile. Reba would be. And it wasn't beyond the bounds of possibility that Barry would eventually turn back to her when he was tired of playing the field. Men like Barry could make paragons of husbands simply because they'd 'been there, done that' and no longer had any hankerings for flirtations. If Paul hadn't married her so young. . . Andie sighed with regret, but more for him than herself. She wondered what he was doing now, whether he would try to find her, how genuine his professed need of her really was. . .

Reba had not noticed her reverie; she was lost in thoughts of her own. Eventually she finished her tea and said, 'Love's a funny thing, Andie. I know I'm crazy to be in love with a man like Barry, but I can't help it.' She reached across the table and squeezed Andie's hand. 'This might sound stupid, but I feel better knowing he's with you rather than with anyone else.'

Andie smiled sadly and squeezed her hand back. 'I'm sorry, Reba.'

Reba rose. 'Enjoy yourself, Andie. Don't feel guilty because of me. I shouldn't have unburdened myself, not to you—it wasn't fair. Let's forget it, shall we?'

'Of course.'

Reba crossed the office to the roster pinned to the wallboard. 'Your first weekend off. Got any plans?'

'Only to relax, write some letters and catch up with my laundry! I might play tennis, and I might go down to the pool for a swim.'

'And hope we don't have a major emergency,' said Reba, pulling a face. 'Gee, I'll never forget that day you arrived. Talk about being dumped in at the deep end! It's a wonder you didn't turn right round and go back.'

'I was tempted to,' Andie said, but did not admit that it would have been for a quite different reason.

'I must say you've fitted in very well,' Reba said generously.

'I didn't think I would, but I do like it here,' Andie admitted. 'I don't even mind the heat.'

'Or the flies?'

Andie waved her hand in front of her face, shooing an imaginary fly—there was seldom an insect in the hospital. 'Oh, I learned the great Australian wave pretty quickly!'

Reba considered her thoughtfully. 'You're a city girl, Andie. They don't usually stick it for long up here. It's too remote.'

'That doesn't bother me. It's strange really, I don't miss the city at all.' Andie was surprised at herself.

'Maybe you're one of those "home is where my tent is" people,' Reba laughed.

Andie joined her amusement. 'Maybe!'

'You ought to see a bit more of the country,' Reba suggested. 'The Flinders Ranges are scenically marvellous. You must ask Cam to take you up to Marshall's Creek some time—it's a very special spot.'

'I wouldn't dream of suggesting it. . .' Andie wished her tone had been less sharp.

Reba gave her a speculative look. 'I thought you and he got on well.'

'As colleagues,' Andie said. 'Neither of us is interested in any relationship beyond that.'

It was a pleasant prospect, having a whole weekend off. Andie went home that Friday evening with a light heart and a determination to catch up on all the things she had neglected lately. And also to just relax. She hadn't seen Barry for a day or two, and he was probably unaware that she had the weekend off. She had no intention of letting him know. Maybe, she thought, he was cooling off already. The possibility gave her a sense of relief, not because he pressured her, which he didn't, but because of Reba. Why couldn't Barry see what a marvellous wife Reba would make?

Andie made herself a quick snack of baked beans on toast, and sat down at the kitchen table to eat it. She had just cleared the plate when the doorbell rang.

Barry, she thought, without enthusiasm, and went reluctantly to answer it.

'Cam. . .' Andie had not expected him. She'd seen even less of him than Barry that week, and she knew it was his weekend off too. 'I thought you'd have left for Marshall's Creek by now.'

He hovered in the doorway. 'I'm not going till tomorrow morning. May I come in?'

She stood aside. 'Yes. Yes, of course.' Her heartbeat quickened. He looked like a man with something to say, and she feared it was going to be about Paul and her again. She wasn't sure if she could stand any more of that. She led the way to the kitchen. 'I've just finished my tea. I was going to make some coffee. Would you like a cup?'

'Thanks.' He pulled out a kitchen chair and sank on to it.

Andie put the kettle on and rattled cups and saucers. Waiting for the kettle to boil, she looked at him questioningly. 'This isn't just a social call—am I right?'

His eyes slowly drifted over her in a thoughtful way. Andie had changed into an over-large pink and yellow striped surf shirt and yellow shorts. She had unpinned her hair and it hung uncombed about her shoulders. She looked almost as young as she had in London, Cam thought. That air of innocent youthfulness had not deceived him then, and he must not let it deceive him now. So what was he doing here? It had been an impulse he had obeyed without thinking, born of a desire to be fair, perhaps. He'd been a bit rough on her. What? She'd lied, hadn't she? Was he going soft in his middle age? Or was it just that he wanted the truth from her, a truth that matched what Paul had told him? Reassurance for his own conscience. . .

He smiled at her. 'It is a social call, Andie, but I did come for a special reason. I was wondering if you'd like to come up to Marshall's Creek this weekend.'

Andie's eyes widened. Had Reba said something? she wondered. Surely she wouldn't have asked him to invite her. 'Why?' she asked.

He wasn't prepared for the question. 'Because you haven't seen much of the country around here yet, have you? There's some magnificent scenery in this northern part of the Ranges.'

'So Reba was telling me, only today,' Andie said, but he did not bat an eyelash. Nevertheless, she asked suspiciously, 'Was this her idea?'

Cam looked amazed. 'Reba's? You mean did she suggest I ought to take you sightseeing?' He chuckled. 'No, Andie, I thought of it all by myself.'

Again she asked, 'Why?'

'Stop being so suspicious! I have no ulterior motive. You'll be adequately chaperoned. My manager and his wife live in the homestead, and there's also a ranger.'

Andie flushed from annoyance. 'I certainly wasn't suggesting. . .'

Cam linked his fingers and rested his chin on them. His mouth twisted slightly, a small muscular movement, not a smile. 'Let's just say it's by way of apologising for slamming into you the other night.'

'But not because you've decided to believe me?' Pride made her sound distant and cool.

He regarded her stonily. 'You know I can't,' he said quietly.

'Well, why invite me up to your place? If you still think I'm a liar, I wonder you can stand the sight of me!'

'Andie,' he said warningly, 'don't fly off the handle again. I know we have an impasse over Paul, but can't we just accept that?'

'No, of course we can't.' Andie ran her tongue over her bottom lip and then bit hard into it. This was ridiculous.

Cam rose. 'Yes, I suppose it was stupid of me to ask you. If you don't want to come, that's OK.'

'I didn't say that. . .' She swallowed hard. It was only natural he'd believe Paul rather than her. 'Of course I'd love to see where you live, but. . .' Would it make any difference? she wondered. Was this her chance to convince him that she hadn't lied? Would she regret it if she didn't take the opportunity suddenly offered?

His dark eyes were steady, hard but not cold. 'It's up to you.'

'I—I had a few things I planned to do this weekend. It's the first full two-day break I've had.'

'You can phone Barry and tell him you'll be out of town,' Cam said, with the faintest of mocking smiles.

Andie lifted her chin. 'I wasn't planning to see Barry, as it happens. I was going to write letters, do my laundry, relax. . .'

The twitch at the corners of his mouth turned into a real smile. 'You can write your letters at Marshall's Creek if you want, and relax as much as you like. You can even bring your laundry and let Moira run it through the washing machine for you.'

'Who's Moira?' she asked.

'My manager's wife, Moira Patterson. Her husband is Derek.'

'I suppose the laundry could wait,' Andie said slowly.

Cam was surprised at how pleased he felt at her capitulation, reluctant though it was. 'So you'll come?'

Andie moistened her lips again. She wasn't sure that she was doing the right thing, but the temptation to go was too strong. 'Yes, why not?' she said airily. 'You might not ask me again if I refuse now, and who else is going to show me the Flinders Ranges if you don't?'

He had to curb the stretch of his smile. His pleasure puzzled him. Here was the woman who had betrayed his brother, and he was actually looking forward to spending the weekend in her company. He must be mad.

'Be ready about six,' he told her. 'I like to get an early start when I don't leave until Saturday. The weekend is all too short as it is.'

'Let's hope you don't get called back for an emergency this time,' Andie said.

He nodded ruefully. 'Let's hope Barry's beeper is working!'

'What do I bring—I mean, to wear?' she asked.

He looked a bit puzzled. 'To wear? Oh, just casual gear. What you've got on's fine—jeans, a sweater or cardigan. It can be chilly at night. Have you got any sturdy shoes? We might go bush-walking.'

'I've got good trainers,' she told him.

'They'll do. We won't go far.' He realised that he was beginning to sound enthusiastic.

Andie smiled. 'Thanks, Cam. I'm looking forward to it.'

He started towards the door. 'Thanks for the tea. See you at six.'

'I'll set my alarm!'

When he had gone, Andie sank on to a chair and

gripped the table edge, hardly able to believe what had just happened. She still didn't understand why he had asked her, and she understood even less why she had accepted. She was crazy, imagining she could persuade him to believe her story rather than Paul's. Paul was his brother, after all.

Just try and enjoy the weekend, she told herself soberly.

When Cam reached the house, the telephone was ringing. It was his ranger. 'Hi, Fritz. Yeah, tomorrow morning, usual time. Everything OK?' The ranger's reply brought a frown to his forehead. 'Damn!' Cam exploded. 'I've arranged to bring someone for the weekend. . .' He ran his fingers through his already unruly hair, only half listening to what the ranger was saying. He said absently, 'Right, see you. Cheers.'

'Damn!' he said again as he put the phone down. Andie mightn't be too pleased. . . If he told her, she might insist on cancelling the arrangement. He stared at the picture of rugged mountains on the hall wall. He didn't want to cancel. He decided to say nothing.

CHAPTER SIX

ANDIE leaned back in her seat and closed her eyes as the Cessna gathered speed for take-off. With her thumbs jammed inside the seatbelt and her toes clenched, she waited for her stomach to jolt as they left the ground. She had never flown in a plane as small as a Cessna before, but until they had reached the Boobera airfield and she had seen the small white aircraft she hadn't been nervous. Clambering into it and belting herself in, she had suddenly had an attack of the jitters. It was so small, so vulnerable. She wished she hadn't come.

'You can open your eyes now!'

Cam's amused voice penetrated the vacuum she had carefully created in her brain. She hadn't meant him to notice. Chagrined, she turned her head to look at him, and gradually her tension eased. He looked so calm and confident at the controls, just as he did at the wheel of his Range Rover, just as he did in the operating-room.

For several moments he concentrated on bringing the aircraft out of the climb, then said, 'Why didn't you tell me you're afraid of flying?'

Andie was stung. 'I'm not! Well, not usually, not in big planes, but this is bit different.' She stared at the clouds and tried not to think about the mile or so of empty space beneath her. 'How long does it take to get to Marshall's Creek?' she asked.

'It's about an hour's flight, that's all, then a twenty-minute trip by truck to the homestead. But we'll take a detour this morning so I can show you some magnificent scenery.'

'Thanks.' Andie smiled gratefully at him. It would

have been nice, she thought, if they could have met as a doctor and a nurse in a remote country hospital, with no past to cloud their relationship. There were times when she liked Dr Cameron Walters a lot.

Cam said, 'There's a map in the locker. I'll show you where we're going.'

Andie spread the map on her knees. He jabbed a finger at it to show her where they were, and traced a straight line to where they were going. 'But we're going to take a roundabout route.'

'Hey,' she said, in a voice of discovery, 'your place is actually marked on the map!'

'All the cattle stations in this part of the world are,' he told her. 'Mine carries no stock now, but it's still noted as a station. I suspect the cartographers felt the need for something to break up all that emptiness. Names make the country look more populated, even if it isn't. Look, just to the north—there—is Tourmaline. That's Madeleine's place.'

Andie wished he hadn't reminded her about Madeleine. Maybe he was just being cautious, letting her know that Madeleine still figured in his landscape. A little bit of typical male ego showing, she told herself.

'Tell me about Marshall's Creek,' she said. 'Why and when did you turn it into a wildlife sanctuary?'

'When I bought it, it hadn't been a cattle run for years. The land was over-grazed and degraded, and the mining prospectors had been in. This is copper and iron ore country, and uranium. The feral goats were the only wildlife thriving. There's too much degraded land in this country, so I decided to give the natural vegetation and wildlife a chance, to bring back the original habitat as far as possible. It's gradually return-ing to its natural state, I'm pleased to say. When we get good rains, the regrowth of indigenous vegetation is prolific, and the wildlife is flourishing again too.'

'You're a greenie,' Andie remarked, only half teasingly.

'As everyone should be,' he answered gravely, 'if there's going to be a liveable planet left for our descendants.'

She fell silent, sensing an implied rebuke. They were already over the Ranges, and the scenery unfolding below the plane was awesome. There was no cloud and the sky was a dense clear blue, sharply contrasting with the rich red, ochre and brown hues of the rugged mountains, whose highest peaks were bare of any vegetation, weather-worn and formidable. There were parts that reminded her of a moonscape.

'It looks very hostile down there,' she murmured. 'But beautiful too.'

'It's magnificent,' Cam agreed with quiet intensity. 'Not the kind of terrain you'd want to get lost in, though.' He banked the plane slightly and they headed off in a different direction.

'Wilpena Pound coming up,' he said after a few minutes. 'Straight ahead.'

Andie gazed facinated at the ring of mountains surrounding the vast natural amphitheatre. As they flew over it the plane dropped suddenly like a lift, and she looked at Cam in alarm.

'Nothing to worry about,' he reassurred her calmly. 'We just hit an air pocket, that's all. You always get turbulence over the Flinders because of the magnetic properties of the iron, but there's no need to be alarmed, I can fly this crate upside down.'

Andie clutched her stomach. 'You wouldn't?'

Deadpan Cam teased, 'I'm quite good at aerobatics. This is a nice clear bit of sky.'

She blanched and threatened, 'I might be sick.'

He shook with silent laughter. 'We have a supply of paper bags specially for the purpose.'

'You beast!'

He relented. 'All right, I won't show off. Not today, anyway.'

Andie was relieved. For another twenty minutes she continued to stare out of the window, while Cam occasionally pointed out a landmark just below them, or in the distance.

'What's all that white stuff reflecting the sun?' she asked, pointing towards the horizon.

'Salt lakes. Lake Torrens over there, and Lake Frome that way. Way to the north is Lake Eyre.'

'All as dry as a bone, and salt. Amazing!'

'There was once an inland sea,' Cam told her, as he turned the aircraft again. After a few minutes, he told her, 'We'll be landing soon.'

The sun had moved, which meant, Andie realised, that they had come in a huge half-circle. She checked her seatbelt, but did not grip it with her thumbs. She was no longer nervous, and she enjoyed the long smooth glide down to a lower altitude. She drew in a sharp breath, however, when the plane swooped through a valley between walls of harsh red rock that seemed so close that she could have reached out and touched either side. But that was an illusion; they were half a mile away. Momentarily, she visualised crash-landing in this remote rugged country where they might never be found. The thought was chilling, and although Cam's expression was relaxed and he seemed perfectly in control she was glad when they flew out of the narrow valley. Moments later she saw ahead of them a plateau, treeless but covered in low scrub.

Cam was heading straight for it, and the Cessna almost seemed to skim the tree-tops. We're going to crash! Andie thought, her heart in her mouth, and then she saw the landing strip, a long narrow patch of red-brown earth with a windsock at one end and a truck standing nearby. Cam suddenly spoke, but not to Andie.

'G'day, Fritz. Everything OK? Over.'

Out of deafening static came a voice. 'Yeah, Cam. The strip's like a billiard table after the grading.'

The voice was broad Australian with a faint European inflexion. 'Was that Mr Patterson?' Andie asked, wondering about the accent.

'No, Fritz Weber, my ranger.' Cam felt a small pang of guilt because he hadn't told her the true situation.

Moments later Andie was meeting the owner of the voice on the CB radio. Cam landed the Cessna smoothly, and as they taxied to a halt a man walked over to them. He was tall, blond, wearing a broad-brimmed hat, sleeveless shirt and minuscule khaki shorts with frayed hems.

Cam shut down the engine and glanced in amusement at Andie's face. 'Don't get excited! It's not Crocodile Dundee.'

Andie quipped back, 'I didn't imagine you'd be bothered by crocs around here.'

'What we are bothered by,' Cam said grimly, 'is wayward tourists and trespassing shooters and any number of people who don't respect private property. Prospecting for gold and other precious metals and stones is a growing hobby for townies. Fritz is the law and order at Marshall's Creek. He's also a zoologist studying the wildlife.'

He jumped out of the Cessna and had a few seconds' conversation with the ranger, who then went around to help Andie down from her seat. 'Hi there, Sister Somers,' he greeted her, smiling, and with candid approval in his eyes. 'Nice to meet you.' He looked amused about something, which made Andie feel uneasy. Did she have lipstick on her teeth? 'Nice to meet you too, Mr Weber,' she said, shaking hands.

'Fritz,' he insisted. He turned to Cam, who had joined them. 'Good trip?'

'Yep. Not much turbulence, so Andie's her normal colour and her breakfast is still with her.'

Fritz laughed. 'Aren't you keen on flying, Sister?'

'I've never flown in a small plane before. It was
quite an experience,' she admitted. 'Cam gave me a
magnificent sightseeing tour.' She smiled. 'My name's
Andie, by the way.'

He grinned. 'Sure.'

While his ranger's eyes lingered on her face, Cam
said briskly, 'Let's get the luggage and go.'

Andie felt a sudden tension in the air and was
puzzled. The two men seemed friendly enough, and
Cam had spoken highly of Fritz.

They transferred her bag and Cam's to the truck,
then efficiently secured the Cessna's wheels and wings
with chocks and ropes attached to pegs in the ground
so that the plane could not capsize in a high wind.
Fritz took the wheel of the Toyota and Cam motioned
Andie to get in beside him. He squeezed in next to
her, and in a cloud of dust they roared off down a
narrow wheel-rutted track into the bush.

For several miles they were hemmed in by sheer,
jagged cliffs of orange, red and ochre rock which
towered above like primordial skyscrapers. It was
desolate, yet awesomely beautiful. The track was
rough and they were jolted up and down and from side
to side every few seconds. Andie was thrown time and
again hard up against Cam, then back hard against
Fritz, her shoulders and thighs rubbing theirs. Once
she caught a sultry sidelong look from Fritz. He was
enjoying it! There was no such provocative look from
Cam, though.

For most of the journey Fritz gave them a commen-
tary on an incident with a group of tourists he had
permitted to camp on the property. They had become
drunk and rowdy and he had had a bad time turning
them off.

'Some naturalists' club!' he snorted in disgust. 'They
probably wouldn't have known spinifex from
stinkweed!'

Andie was beginning to feel nauseated by the jolting

and the dust which seeped even into the sealed cabin, so she didn't follow the story too well. Cam and Fritz conversed across the top of her head, and she wished Fritz would keep his eyes on the track and not keep turning his head and taking both hands off the wheel to make a point. There were endless bends in the road and sometimes sheer drops on one side, but Fritz drove as though they were late for an important appointment. They were going to be too early for the ultimate appointment, Andie thought with grim resignation, if he didn't pay more attention to his driving. It was far more hair-raising, she reflected, than flying in a small plane!

At last the homestead came into view. It was a stone-built verandaed building with a cluster of outbuildings nearby. It was hemmed in by hills and shaded by tall gum trees. The Toyota roared into the yard and stopped in another cloud of red dust. Andie tumbled out after Cam and was almost knocked over by a huge exuberant dog who dashed around a corner of the house and flung himself at her, barking joyously.

'Nargun, *down!*' Cam's command brought instant obedience from the hound, who looked like a cross between a German Shepherd and a Rottweiler, or something equally absurd.

The dog abandoned Andie and flung himself at Cam with the same degree of enthusiastic welcome. Cam made a big fuss of the animal and quietened him.

Lifting the bags from the back of the Toyota, Fritz said to Andie, 'He's just excitable. He never bites.'

Andie, breathless from the onslaught, laughed. 'I'm glad to hear it. He looks as though he could take a week's dinners in one chomp! Don't worry, I love dogs. He winded me, that's all.'

Cam, who had started ahead of them, turned round at the sound of Andie's and Fritz's laughter. He might have known Fritz would flirt with her, and that she'd like it. He ground his heel into the dirt, surprised at the resentment he felt, and called, 'Are you two coming inside?'

They caught up with him at the veranda. There was no sign yet of the manager and his wife, which struck Andie as a little odd.

'I'll put your bag in the guest room,' Fritz said, opening the door, and motioning her to go in. Halfway along the passage, he pushed open another door, dumped her case, and said to Cam, 'I'll be in the cabin till lunchtime if you want me, and out on the south boundary this afternoon and tonight. We've had a few spotlighters on the ridge picking off the wallabies.'

Cam nodded. 'OK.'

Fritz winked at Andie and departed. Meanwhile a suspicion had been forming in Andie's mind. 'The Pattersons?' she queried. 'Where are they?'

Cam faced the moment of truth. 'They had to leave in a hurry. Moira's mother in Adelaide was taken ill and Derek drove her down.'

'When?' she asked tautly.

'Yesterday.'

She moistened her lips. 'You knew that when you asked me to come up this weekend. What's the score, Cam?'

'I didn't know, not until after I'd talked to you. Fritz rang last night.'

'You could still have cancelled the trip,' she pointed out.

'Why? It seemed a pity, especially as I have no intention of molesting you. I didn't want you to cry off just because you didn't trust me, or you were afraid it might look provocative if you came.'

His directness stung. Andie felt a little foolish, but she was still mad at him. 'You could have told me,' she repeated.

He smiled mockingly. 'You can have a key to your door if you insist.'

A clock in another room chimed as they faced each other, sparks still flying. Andie counted the strokes.

'I could always get Fritz to fly you back,' Cam suggested. He made it sound like a monstrous imposition, and his tone derided her.

Andie wasn't sure how to take all this. She had been astonished enough at his inviting her in the first place. The new twist made her feel doubly uncomfortable. She'd known it was a mistake to come.

Cam set off down the passageway. 'Let's have a cup of coffee,' he suggested calmly.

She followed him into the kitchen, which to her surprise was spacious, modern and attractive, with pine cupboards and cream Formica tops. There was a large wood-burning stove, a refrigerator and a pine table and chairs. Cam opened the fridge and contemplated the contents.

'Well, we won't starve.' He turned to grin at Andie. 'Are you a good cook? I'm not over-fond of baked beans.'

She gritted her teeth for a moment, then laughed. 'So that's why you didn't put me off. You wanted someone to cook your Sunday lunch!'

Her laughter was a relief. Cam joined in, and said, 'That's about the strength of it.'

She crossed to where she could see an electric kettle standing beside the stainless steel sink. 'Let's have that coffee, shall we?'

Her face was slightly flushed, and strands of blonde hair had escaped from the ponytail into which she'd scraped it. The pale green T-shirt moulded her small firm breasts and her white cotton shorts emphasised long, smoothly tanned legs. As she filled the kettle, her back towards him, Cam found his eyes drawn to the provocative line of her thighs, the tantalising faintly blue-veined hollows behind her knees, and he felt a strong desire to reach out for her. He shoved his hands in his pockets to prevent it.

'I'll be on the veranda,' he said, and escaped.

Andie shrugged. Cam was too accustomed to being waited on. Jean and the Pattersons quite clearly spoiled him. She stood with her hands on her hips waiting for the kettle to boil, and with the feeling that she'd been deliberately manoeuvred into doing likewise.

After she'd finished her coffee, she left Cam with the pot and returned to the kitchen to make lunch. She hadn't asked Cam where he liked to eat, the dining-room or the kitchen, so she went back to the veranda. He was not there. She called through the house, but he was not inside either. She assumed he must have gone over to see Fritz.

She went out the back and scanned the yard, shading her eyes against the sun with her hand. Some distance from the homestead, sheltered by trees, was a log cabin. She was about to stroll over to it when she spotted the gong. It was a large metal oil-drum lid suspended from the veranda rafter, and there was a thick piece of wood on a rope hanging beside it.

She struck the gong hard with the wood. The sound startled a flock of pink and grey galahs which expoded noisily from the nearest gum tree. A few minutes later Cam came into the kitchen. He had changed into faded old green shorts and an unbuttoned fawn shirt, and his physical impact on Andie was stronger than ever.

'Where do you want to eat?' she asked.

He slumped into a kitchen chair. 'Here's fine.'

Andie set two places, then put a plate of salad in front of him, and sat down opposite.

'I noticed you have quite a thriving vegetable garden,' she remarked. 'Where does the water come from?'

'There are a lot of springs in this area. We have an underground supply which is pretty reliable, nevertheless we try not to waste it. One wash-up a day will do,

Four Irresistible
Temptations
FREE!

PLUS A MYSTERY GIFT

Temptations offer you all the age-old passion and tenderness of romance, now experienced through very contemporary relationships.

And to introduce to you this powerful and highly charged series, we'll send you **four Temptation romances** absolutely **FREE** when you complete and return this card.

We're so confident that you'll enjoy Temptations that we'll also reserve a subscription to our Reader Service, for you; which means that you'll enjoy...

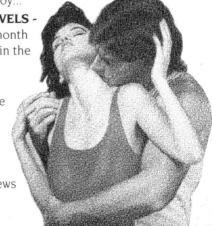

- ❧ **FOUR BRAND NEW NOVELS -** sent direct to you each month (before they're available in the shops).

- ❧ **FREE POSTAGE AND PACKING -** we pay all the extras.

- ❧ **FREE MONTHLY NEWSLETTER -** packed with special offers, competitions, authors news and much more...

CLAIM THESE GIFTS OVERLEAF

Free Books Certificate

A Free Gift

Return this card now and we'll send you this cuddly Teddy Bear absolutely FREE together with...

A Mystery Gift

We all love mysteries, so as well as the FREE Teddy Bear there's an intriguing FREE gift specially for you.

YES! Please send me **four FREE Temptations** together with my **FREE gifts.** Please also reserve a special Reader Service subscription for me. If I decide to subscribe, I will receive four Temptation romances each month for just £7.00 postage and packing free. If I decide not to subscribe I shall write to you within 10 days. The free books and gifts are mine to keep in any case. **I understood that I am under no obligation whatsoever.** I may cancel or suspend my subscription at any time simply by writing to you. I am over 18 years of age.

MS/MRS/MISS/MR _____

ADDRESS _____

_____

POSTCODE _____ SIGNATURE _____

7A2T

and try to be economical under the shower. All our
waste water is piped straight to the vegetable garden.'

'I presume you also have your own power?'

'Yes. We have a generator for electricity, and Fritz
chops wood for the stove.'

Andie served the rock melon she had sliced with a
scoop of vanilla ice-cream in each hollow. Cam said. 'I
thought we might do a boundary ride this afternoon.'

'Ride?' she queried. 'You have horses?' She had
never ridden one.

'Trail-bikes. They cost less to feed!' He was amused
at her dismay. 'Don't worry, they're dead easy to
handle. You can ride a push-bike, can't you?'

'Yes, of course.'

'I'll show you,' he said. 'Nothing to it. The gears are
very simple.'

On Cam's instructions, Andie packed a large
Thermos and some cake, and shortly after lunch they
set off. Andie's training period had been brief, a few
circuits of the yard to learn how to control the trail-
bike, which skill she mastered quickly, much to her
own pride and Cam's evident satisfaction.

Exploring the country on the ground was an exhil-
arating experience, and, although the humps and
bumps of the rough terrain shook every bone in her
body so that she wondered if she would ever sleep that
night, she enjoyed every minute.

Sometimes they could ride side by side, sometimes
it was necessary to go single file. Cam shouted the
names of birds to her and occasionally stopped to point
out some unusual plant or flower. Eventually they
caught up with Fritz, who had been tracking wallabies.
He was scanning a huge outcrop of red rocks with
binoculars. Cam motioned to Andie to cut the engine
of the bike and they dismounted some distance from
the ranger.

'We don't want to disturb them,' he explained in a
low tone.

Fritz greeted them briefly, then handed the binoculars to Andie. 'Take a sweep across from that bent gum,' he said. 'They're on the big flat rock and some of the ledges behind.'

Cam said, 'These are the yellow-footed rock wallabies. We thought they were extinct in this area, so it's great to know they're still around.'

'And people try to shoot them?' asked Andie, aghast.

'Some yobbos do.'

'But aren't they protected?'

Cam and Fritz laughed. Cam said, 'By law, yes, but in reality only by vigilantes like Fritz.'

The shadows were already lengthening as the sun dipped towards the higher peaks, and Cam soon suggested they start moving again. Judging by the tent pitched nearby, Fritz was camping out tonight, Andie concluded. Which meant she would be all alone with Cam.

Back at the homestead, she showered and began to prepare dinner. When Cam suddenly appeared in the kitchen doorway, he startled her. She caught her breath as she looked up at him lounging there, a lazy smile on his lips. His hair was still damp and curling around his collar line and over his forehead. He was wearing pale blue linen shorts and a short-sleeved white shirt. He looked excessively handsome—more than she wanted him to. The open shirt gave her glimpses of dark chest hair arrowing to the waistband of his shorts. She looked quickly away, alarmed at the way her heart had suddenly started pounding.

'Nearly ready,' she said, ironing out the tremor in her voice with difficulty. He was a powerful presence and no mistake.

'Like a drink?' he asked.

'I wouldn't mind.'

'Scotch, gin, brandy, sherry?'

'There's a cask of white wine in the fridge. May I have a glass of that?'

'Whatever you like.'

He vanished briefly to fetch glasses and a bottle of whisky from the dining-room buffet. When he came back and busied himself taking the wine cask and a tray of ice from the fridge, then pouring the drinks, Andie was acutely conscious of his movements behind her as he strode back and forth across the narrow kitchen, and she chopped parsley. She'd been closer to him in the operating-room, but here the atmosphere was more highly charged with a different kind of tension.

Cam downed his drink and said, 'Shall we eat on the veranda?'

'That'd be nice,' Andie agreed.

A full moon rose while they were eating, its sudden appearance startling her. The enormous deep orange orb looked so unreal rising over the dark mountains, almost as though it was a stage effect.

'It's very peaceful here,' Andie said softly. 'It's no wonder you like to get away up here often.'

Cam smiled. 'I can't say Boobera Hospital's exactly frenetic, except on rare occasions, like the day you arrived. I have a pretty easy time of it, really. I was lucky to get a post so near to Marshall's Creek. Grandfather's money doesn't pay all the bills, I'm afraid.'

'Would he have approved of your spending your inheritance this way?' she enquired.

'Definitely.' He added, 'He was a doctor too, you know. Paul must have told you.'

Andie was surprised. 'No, he didn't. He didn't talk much about his family.' She wished Cam hadn't mentioned Paul.

'Except me,' Cam said ironically. 'He's still very bitter because he's been denied his share of Grandfather's money until he's thirty.'

Andie felt a tug of loyalty. 'Well, it was a bit unfair,' she said.

'Was it?' He looked steadily at her. 'Grandfather knew Paul was inclined to be impulsive. He hoped that by the time he was thirty he'd be more stable and sensible, and not waste his inheritance. That's why he insisted that he could only inherit earlier if he married and I considered the match would be a stable relationship.' He smiled faintly. 'Grandfather was a great believer in the power of a good woman!'

'Yes, I know, you told me!' said Andie, feeling on edge. 'But in your opinion I wasn't, was I, Cam?' She shot an accusing look at him, and rose from the table to stand at the veranda railing looking at the moon. She had wanted to make him believe the truth about her and Paul, but now suddenly she didn't want to talk about it. It was spoiling everything.

She felt a hand slide across her waist. 'Andie. . .'

'I don't want to talk about Paul,' she said fiercely. 'I don't want to talk like we did the other night.' She turned to him angrily. 'Is that why you brought me here this weekend? To castigate me all over again?'

With her striking blonde hair loose, she looked breathtakingly lovely in the moonlight, Cam was thinking. He lifted a wayward strand of her hair and tucked it behind her ear, lightly caressing the soft curve of flesh and moving his fingers involuntarily along her jawline. Her skin felt like satin and he felt her quiver to his touch. Her lips parted slightly and she ran her tongue nervously over them. Her breathing was betrayingly irregular.

'You won't get me to admit the truth you want to believe,' she said raggedly, 'because I've already told you the real truth.'

The temptation to believe her was strong. The temptation to kiss her was even stronger, and the astonishing thing was, he was almost certain she wouldn't object. Emotions stronger than her outward antipathy towards him were surfacing, and to Cam this was a source of wonderment and quiet exultation. But if he tried to seduce her now, because he had deceived her about the Pattersons, she would accuse him of arranging the whole thing on purpose.

'And I almost believe you,' he murmured, bending to kiss her mouth lingeringly but forcing himself not to take it any further. 'You look so beguiling in the moonlight, a man could believe anything you say.'

Andie, her lips burning from the contact with his, jerked angrily away. 'Except the truth!' She turned to face him again. His distrust was hurting more than ever now. 'Cam, I wasn't lying—I swear I wasn't. Why won't you believe me?' Emotion made her voice tremble.

He came close again and fitted his hands around her waist, almost encircling it. 'I try not to do things against my better judgement.'

'But you haven't let me explain properly.'

He took her hand and drew her back to the table. He tipped a little more wine into their glasses. 'All right—explain now,' he invited tersely.

This was what Andie had wanted, the chance to convince him, but now it had come she wasn't so sure. Cam's implacable expression warned her that he would not be easy to persuade. Because he was attracted to her, in spite of himself, she was sure, that was going to make it even harder. He wasn't the kind of man to let mere sensuality cloud his judgement.

She took a deep breath. 'I willingly admit that five years ago I was young and foolish and bowled over by Paul. I didn't know about the inheritance at first, and I was astounded when you objected to our getting married. Of course Paul then told me why, and I was deeply hurt by some of the things you said.You accused me of being a grasping little gold-digger, but I wasn't, and the insult made me angry, so angry I was determined to marry Paul come hell or high water, and make you eat your words. I told myself the inheritance was his and you had no right to interfere. I really hated you for giving me the thumbs down.'

'You called me arrogant and domineering,' he recalled. 'You said I took a fiendish delight in bullying my younger brother.'

Andie blushed and looked into her lap. That was how Paul had painted him, and that was how she had seen him then.

Cam went on quietly, 'I had to consider the possibility that you both might be marrying for the wrong reasons, just so you could get your hands on the money. I didn't want to deprive Paul, but I had an obligation to discharge.'

She refused to concede that. 'Paul was in love with me, Cam, I know he was, and I was head over heels in love with him.'

He flinched at this admission. It shocked him that he didn't want her to have been in love with Paul. 'Why couldn't you have waited until you'd finished your training to get married? That was all I asked, and a testing year of marriage.'

Andie bit her lip. That had been a bone of contention between her and Paul. Paul would not wait; he'd wanted her to give up nursing and get married right away. He had been confident Cam would have to approve once it was a *fait accompli*. In the end she had agreed to compromise: she would marry him right away if he let her continue nursing. But once they were married, Paul had wanted to go home. Cam had gone, and he still had to be persuaded to release Paul's legacy. Andie told Cam all this and he listened without comment.

'I suppose it was foolish of me,' she said soberly. 'Letting him go home without me was asking for trouble, wasn't it? But I only had a few months of my training to go. I owed it to my brothers, who'd paid my way, to finish. By the time I arrived in Sydney, things were already starting to go wrong. You were still adamant about not approving of our marriage and Paul was getting more and more impatient. We started having small quarrels, then bigger ones, and finally I discovered he was seeing other women.'

'Eventually he told me he was leaving me for a woman called Diana, who was having his child, and he wanted a divorce as quickly as possible so he could marry her.' Andie stared for a moment into her wine, then lifted her eyes to Cam's wondering how he would take her next revelation. 'I think he hoped you might relent if there was a child involved.'

'You mean, it was deliberate?' Cam looked shocked.

She wished the conversation had never started. 'I don't know. . .'

'This is fantasy,' he said slowly. 'Pure fantasy.'

She leaned towards him, desperation in her eyes. 'Cam, it isn't—it's true.'

'But he didn't marry the woman.' His scepticism was scathing.

'I didn't know he hadn't until recently, when he contacted me. . .'

Cam's eyebrows shot up. 'Paul contacted you? Recently?'

'Yes. It seems that Diana miscarried, then broke it off with him. It seems he never told you about her.'

'Why did he get in touch with you after so long?' he asked suspiciously.

Andie wasn't prepared to reveal everything. She shrugged. 'He was at a loose end, I suppose; between girlfriends, maybe.'

Cam asked slowly, 'Did Paul send you up here?'

Her mouth fell open. 'No! Cam, you can't think. . .?'

He framed his face in his hands for a moment. 'Sometimes I'm not sure what I think.'

It was all becoming too much for her. Her control was slipping. 'Paul didn't send me here,' she whis-

pered. 'I had no idea you were here. It was just
coincidence.' She buried her face in her hands and
wept. She'd gone through the pain of telling him in
detail, and still he doubted her.

'Andie, don't. . . .'

She wasn't aware he had moved until he pulled her
to her feet and folded his arms tightly around her. His
voice was husky. 'I want to believe you. I almost do. I
know Paul's weaknesses, although I try not to be too
hard on him. I've only ever done what I thought was
for the best, but now I'm not sure that it always was.
If I'd given my consent to your marriage, perhaps
you'd still be together now.'

His fingers threaded through her hair, caressing her
nape and stroking her back soothingly. Andie clung to
him for comfort, and found it despite everything.
When he slid his thumbs under her chin and tilted her
face so that her mouth was within reach of his, she
parted her lips involuntarily, and let him kiss her.
Although she had been Paul's wife, she had never
experienced so strong a desire as she was experiencing
now. Cam's potent masculinity seemed to touch every
centimetre of her skin, penetrate every corner of her
being, awakening sensations that had never even
existed before. A long pleasurable shiver ran through
her and she pressed closer, letting him mould her body
to his, feeling the strength and hardness of his muscles,
responding to the urgency of his caress.

Suddenly he lifted his mouth from hers and looked
into her eyes for a long moment. Finally he murmured,
'I think we have a complication here, Sister Somers.
What do you think is the best treatment?'

Andie knew what he wanted her to say, and it was
hard not to say it. Her whole being cried out for the
solace of love and fulfilment, but she knew she mustn't
give in to it. One brother had made a mess of her life,
and she wasn't going to risk having the other do
likewise. Breathlessly, she answered, 'I think you may

have made a wrong diagnosis, Dr Walters. There's no complication. All the patients need in this case are private rooms.' She pulled away, smiling to preserve the lightness that she hoped would defuse the situation. 'Goodnight, Cam.'

CHAPTER SEVEN

'How was your weekend?' asked Reba, first thing on Monday morning when Andie walked in.

'Fine.' The truth was Andie was still feeling over-wrought. She hadn't slept much on Saturday night or last night. Cam had flown them back at dawn today, and it was barely an hour since she'd left him.

Reba had a teasing look. 'How was Marshall's Creek?' She chuckled when Andie looked startled. 'Come on, Andie, you've been in Boobera long enough to know that everything you do is noticed.'

Andie sighed. 'All right. I went to Marshall's Creek with Cam. I had a great weekend. We went boundary riding on trail-bikes, swimming in the waterhole, and Madeleine Trentham came over on Sunday evening. She and Fritz and Cam and I played bridge!'

Reba's eyebrows shot up. 'I wonder who told her you were there alone with Cam?'

'How did you know. . .?'

'That the Pattersons had gone off in a hurry on Friday afternoon to visit Moira's sick mother in Adelaide? Bill Clarke, our local plumber. They chartered his plane. Barry sent Bill down for a chest X-ray on Saturday morning, and we had to talk about something!'

Andie pulled a face. 'There's just no privacy in this town.'

'I think Barry was a bit put out because you'd skived off without telling him,' Reba said, with a glint in her eye. 'Serves him right!'

Andie grimaced. Reba's philosophical approach to romance was remarkable. If she was jealous of the other women Dr Lester took out, she never showed it.

'He took me to a film,' Reba said smugly, 'and I slapped his face for trying to get fresh. That man has a few things to learn about manners. And women!'

'Good for you!' Andie said with feeling. Perhaps she should have slapped Cam's face—on Friday as well as on Saturday. But if she'd done so on Friday, there would have been no Saturday. Or Sunday. And despite everything, she had enjoyed her weekend—in parts.

Reba was frowning at the roster. 'Andie, I'd like you to keep an eye on the men's ward as well today. I've only got Lenore and Jessica there. And could you possibly do a night shift? Linda's sick again with a migraine. They last two or three days with her. Tonight, and tomorrow as well, I expect.' She glanced at Andie apologetically. 'You could go off earlier this afternoon and get some shut-eye. Nights aren't usually onerous, just a bit long.'

'I don't mind.' Andie agreed readily to the request.

'You haven't got a date?'

'Definitely not.'

Reba was relieved. 'Thanks. What I'd give to be able to phone an agency for a temp. Jiggering about with the roster is a nightmare!'

Andie went off to find Lenore, and together they laid up a trolley and a short time later entered the men's ward to take routine observations and give out medications where they were due.

'Your temp's up a bit today, Mr Guthrie,' Andie said, shaking the thermometer she had just removed from the mouth of the first patient on their list. 'We'll have to see what we can do to get it down again.' The patient had been operated on for gallstones, successfully, but his general condition was giving cause for some concern. There did not seem to be any obvious reason for fever.

'I always was hot stuff!' joked Mr Guthrie, whose reputation for philandering with nurses was well known. Andie glanced at Lenore, who rolled her eyes at the ceiling.

'Well, at your age,' Andie told him deadpan, 'it's a bit risky. I'm afraid we'll have to cool you down.'

'Shall I tell you what'd really cool me down quick?' said Mr Guthrie with a grin.

Andie groaned silently. She had asked for that. 'No.'

He winked broadly. 'I was only thinking of a nice cold schooner of lager, Sister.'

His innocent tone made Lenore crack up, and Andie let herself be the butt of the joke. She supervised Lenore entering all the obs on Mr Guthrie's chart, then they moved on to the next bed. The patient had just returned from the bathroom and was struggling out of his dressing-gown.

'Mr Thompson! What are you doing back with us?' Andie exclaimed. 'Your leg's barely healed. Are you back at work?'

'Not yet.' He looked sheepish. 'I had another little accident, Sister, on Saturday. I was lopping a couple of trees for a mate and I cut me foot.' He lifted it to show her. 'Dr Lester said I'd better have a couple of days in bed.'

'You should call for a wheelchair when you want to go to the toilet, Mr Thompson,' she said. 'You shouldn't be walking about on your foot.'

'I didn't want to bother anyone,' he explained.

She was puzzled by the look on his face and the contortions he was going through to remove the dressing-gown. It was as though his arm was injured as well as his foot. She helped him to get his right arm free. He stretched out on the bed, and she noticed how he winced when lifted his arm to pull himself up on the pillows.

'Is your arm painful?' she asked. 'Have you injured that too?'

'No, it's nothing—just a twinge. Must have strained it larking about up them trees, I suppose.'

Andie gave him his insulin injection, wrote up his chart, then paused thoughtfully. She caught hold of his wrist and elbow and slowly raised his arm. 'Does that hurt?' she asked.

'Not when you're holding it.' He seemed surprised.

'But it does when you raise it by yourself?' The patient nodded, and Andie continued to lift his arm a little further, then she said, 'Now stretch up above your head,' and let go.

Dean Thompson complied. 'Don't hurt like that, Sister. It's just some ways I move the bug. . .beg pardon, move me arm. Gives me a jolt, it does, sometimes.'

'Try lifting it up with your other hand,' said Andie. 'That'll help. And don't forget, next time you go to the toilet, ask for a wheelchair, OK?'

The ward was only half occupied, so the two nurses finished their task quickly. Andie then despatched Lenore to general tidying up, while she went back to the women's ward. Tending both wards kept her busy and it was almost visiting hours before she found time to go along to Reba's office to consult one of the medical textbooks there. She was anxious to be sure of her ground before she conveyed her conclusions to Cam.

Cam. . . Trying not to think about him was impossible. Andie stood with the book in her hand, her finger on the index, and sighed. She was still feeling confused. Even the normality of Sunday had not altered that. Saturday night had been vividly in her mind all the next day, and she hadn't known how to deal with it. Cam seemed to have no such problem. He had suggested a swim and a picnic lunch at the waterhole, a couple of miles from the homestead, and, so as not to betray her real feelings, Andie had readily agreed. What were her real feelings anyway? Suddenly she wasn't sure any more.

It had only been a short ride to the waterhole, but

the sun was hot and she had been more than ready to
cool off when they arrived. She had run over the rocks
to the edge, looking eagerly down into the still mirror
surface of the water, which looked very inviting. The
waterhole was a deep hollow between rugged red cliffs
with ghost gums sprouting even out of clefts in their
steep sides.

'Race you to the other side,' said Cam, coming up
behind her. He began to strip off his khaki shirt and
trousers. Andie felt a little nervous about exposing her
body, but she could hardly dive in fully clothed! She
peeled off her top and shorts, and glancing towards
him saw that he was watching. Her throat constricted
at the sight of his near-nakedness. Without clothing to
conceal his torso, the muscles in his chest and arms
were impressive. A sprinkling of dark hair fuzzed his
chest and arrowed down to the waistband of his black
swim shorts which hung on slim hips between a narrow
waist and sinewy thighs. He could have easily modelled
for a keep-fit advertisement, Andie thought, swallow-
ing hard and averting her gaze. She didn't stop to
wonder whether her slender maillot-clad figure was
having a similar effect on him. She hesitated only a
second on the rocky edge, then arched her body in a
dive.

She heard Cam shout, 'Bravo!' as she went under.
The water was colder than she had expected and she
surfaced gasping. Cam was also in the water and
striking out with a bold, strong overarm for the other
side. Andie set off in pursuit.

She reached the far side of the waterhole only a few
metres behind him. He was clinging to a rock, treading
water, and grinned at her challengingly. 'Not bad!
Let's see if you can beat me back.'

'Wait!' She grabbed breathlessly at the rock just
near him. 'Let me get my breath back!'

'Too cold for you?'

'It was a bit of a shock, but it's fantastic.' Andie

gazed up through the overhanging trees, feeling the
filtered sun on her face with pleasure. 'This beats any
suburban swimming-pool!'

'You said it!' he exclaimed, clearly in his element.

Their eyes met and she felt the same swift sensual
rapport as last night. 'Get ready—go!' she cried, and
shot forward towards the other bank.

Cam won again, of course. 'But only by a short
length!' Andie declared. They clambered out, laughing, and grabbed towels—each other's.

'Hey, this is yours,' said Cam, and flung it around
her, giving her a brisk rub which started the blood
pounding through her veins.

She pushed him away, tossing his towel to him. She
dried herself hurriedly and twisted her damp hair up
into a knot on top of her head. 'Now for lunch.' She
dived for the picnic basket. 'I'm ravenous.'

The food disposed of, they stretched out in the
dappled shade, not talking now, just listening to the
sounds of the bush in quiet contentment. Insects
chirred in the treetops and undergrowth, and birds
flashed back and forth. The fluting notes of the pied
butcher-birds hung on the air like musical jewels, and
Andie felt wonderfully at peace.

'This is a heavenly place,' she sighed drowsily. 'I
could stay here forever.'

Cam murmured a reply she didn't hear. She must
have drifted off, because she woke with a start to find
him tickling her nose with a blade of grass which had a
tip like a fine paintbrush.

'What were you dreaming?' he asked softly.

'I wasn't. . .'

'There was a suggestion of a smile on your lips.'

'Then it must have been about food!'

Cam's eyes were in shadow, but she sensed an
intensity in the way he was looking at her. 'Or love,'
he said softly.

'Now, why would I. . .?'

'Because I. . .' he bent his head and touched his lips to her mouth '. . .kissed you while you were asleep.'

A dangerous warmth was trickling along Andie's veins again. 'Unfair,' she murmured, and tried to roll out of his way, but he dropped a hand on to the rock beyond her and barred her escape.

His closeness had been hard to resist, and she hadn't. She had let him kiss her. It had seemed so right somehow, even though deep down she knew it wasn't, never could be. But there, and then, nothing else had mattered except that being in Cam's arms, feeling the warmth of his skin against hers, midriff to midriff, thigh to thigh, was wonderful. And exquisitely dangerous.

His finger had traced the shape of her nose and mouth, strayed lightly over her skin to the top of her swimsuit and slid under the fabric before she managed to summon the will-power to grasp his hand and firmly remove it.

He looked at her for a moment, then rolled away, lying with his hands folded behind his head. Neither spoke for some minutes, then Cam suggested they have another swim before they left.

As they came out of the water, he dropped a small bombshell. 'Madeleine's coming over after dinner,' he said, and Andie tensed. He turned to smile at her. 'You don't mind?'

She was annoyed to find that she did. 'No, of course not.' Why was it so hard to smile, to sound pleased?

'It's pretty lonely for her over there when there are no guests, and apparently there aren't this weekend. Madeleine likes company.'

'Especially yours,' said Andie, starting to dress, and wishing her remark had not sounded so sharp.

Cam pulled on his shirt and shrugged. 'She was in a mess emotionally when Hugo died. I tried to help her snap out of it. She got to depend on me for a lot of things.'

'Yes, she told me.' Andie kept her face averted as she strapped the picnic basket back on the bike. 'Why didn't you ask her over for dinner?'

He came up close behind and kissed the back of her neck, nuzzling her ear. 'Because two's company.'

She half turned. 'You're as bad as Barry.' She didn't really like the fact that he was flirting with her, and hated having to admit that, in spite of everything, a part of her found him irresistible. . .

'You look serious. What's up?' Reba came in, raising her eyebrows at Andie, and looking questioningly at the textbook.

Andie's thoughts of the weekend receded and she said, 'Oh, I was just looking up something.'

'Yes?' Reba queried. 'Anything I can help with?'

'I—I just want to check a couple of things,' Andie said, not wanting to voice her suspicions until she had at least confirmed that she had grounds for them. 'I'll get out of your way.'

'No need, I'm not stopping long,' said Reba, grabbing a sheaf of papers off her desk. 'Got to see Peg about a few things. Paperwork!' She pulled a face and started going through the papers in front of her.

Andie found what she wanted in the index and turned to the pages listed. A little smile of satisfaction curved her mouth. She was confident enough now to speak to Cam about it.

Reba was going. 'Hold the fort for me, will you, Andie?' she said. 'Shan't be long, and then you can go.'

As she reached the door, it burst open and Cam's considerable frame filled the space. He looked displeased. 'Reba, where the hell's Andie?' he demanded, then spotted her in the corner and exclaimed, 'Ah, there you are!' His expression spelt trouble.

Reba shot Andie a 'what's all this about?' look and departed.

'Yes?' Andie said calmly.

'What are you doing here? Why aren't you looking after your ward?'

She was alarmed. 'What do you mean? What's happened?' She made a move to push past him to go and see what the fuss was all about.

He barred her way and glared. 'I thought I told you Eric Maguire's dog was not to be allowed in the ward.'

'Yes, you did, and I haven't. . .'

'You obviously didn't tell Lenore or Jessica. The bloody hound was careering all over the place, and it jumped at him as he came back from the bathroom and toppled him on to the floor.'

Andie's hand flew to her mouth. 'Oh, no! His leg. . .?' Mr Maguire's right leg was in plaster to the hip, following an accident with a tractor which had rolled over on to him.

'He's OK. But no thanks to you,' stormed Cam. 'We might have a pretty casual approach to some things in this hospital, but an animal in the ward is unhygienic, disruptive and a downright flouting of the rules. I heard the commotion—it's a wonder you didn't hear it down this end—the dog barking, Lenore and Jessica squealing, and Eric blaspheming.'

Andie was beginning to see the funny side, which Cam evidently could not, but she asked anxiously, 'Is Mr Maguire all right?'

'Fortunately, yes. I got him back to bed. No damage, thank goodness.'

'I'm afraid we didn't hear a thing. We are a fair distance away,' Andie said, adding lamely, 'And there's often quite a lot of noise during visiting hours.' She asked, 'Where's the dog now?'

'Tied up outside, where it should have been in the first place. Didn't you tell those girls not to let it in?'

'Of course I did, but they—Eric and Rex, that is— miss each other dreadfully,' Andie explained. 'I sup-

pose he persuaded one of them.' She added boldly,
'Animals are known to aid patient recovery.'

Cam's expression was chilly. 'I know that. I never
said he couldn't see the mutt. He can be wheeled
outside to see Rex. He can chuck sticks and balls for
him on the lawn. Not in the ward! A couple of the
other patients evidently thought it a great amusement
to throw objects for the dog to fetch—mostly biscuits!'

Andie was forming a horrendous but hilarious image
in her mind, and could only say, 'I'm sorry. I don't
know how it happened. I'd better go and see.'

Cam gave her a withering look. 'I suggest you stay
closer to your ward when you're on duty so you know
what's going on. I might not always be on hand to
salvage a situation.'

'I've been looking after both women's and men's
wards today,' she told him. 'And it is visiting hours.'

He was unmoved and glowered again. 'So? If you
were that busy, what were you doing here? Gossiping,
I suppose.'

'No!' Andie was stung. She brandished the medical
textbook. 'As a matter of fact I came to look up
something. And now Reba's with Matron I'm supposed to be holding the fort for her.' Her patience was
becoming strained by Cam's criticism. 'I can't be in
three places at once!' This was hardly the moment to
broach the subject of Dean Thompson's right shoulder,
she decided, anxious to get along to the ward and find
out exactly what had happened.

Cam let her pass without further comment. He
watched her trim little figure march briskly along the
corridor to the other end of the hospital. He hadn't
needed to be so brusque with her, he thought. But he
wasn't in the best frame of mind today. Life had
suddenly become complicated, or was that merely in
his head? One minute he was regretting ever taking
Andie to Marshall's Creek, the next he was indulging
himself remembering how very pleasant it had been.

Did it matter that he found her untrustworthy on the one hand, but utterly desirable on the other?

'Of course it bloody well matters!' he muttered as he stomped off to his office.

Andie found Lenore pouring barley water for Mr Maguire and Jessica mopping up dusty paw-marks from the lino—as ordered by Cam, she presumed. Mr Maguire's son was visiting today. He and most of the other patients and their visitors grinned when she walked in. When Andie asked what had happened, Lenore looked sheepish.

'It just happened, all of a sudden,' the young nurse told her. 'The dog saw Mr Maguire and went straight for him and tried to jump into his arms.'

'Rex is a cattle dog,' Eric Maguire explained. 'He always jumps into my arms when he sees me.'

'But he's not supposed to come into the ward,' Andie scolded. 'You know that, Mr Maguire.' She frowned accusingly at his son, who grinned and tried to look contrite.

'It wasn't the nurses' fault. They said Rex wasn't allowed, but I sneaked him in when they weren't looking.'

'This is my son, Denis,' said Mr Maguire.

Andie nodded and Denis said, 'It was hilarious! When Dad fell over, Rex went berserk, and everybody started shouting at once. Then Dr Walters came in and chased him—Rex, that is—round and round the beds, and finally cornered him under Dad's.'

'It was a scream,' agreed Jessica, failing to keep a straight face any longer. 'Really it was. We were trying to get Mr Maguire back into bed, only he's so heavy with the plaster on, and Denis was chasing the dog, and then Dr Walters came in and Rex took refuge under the bed, and growled when Dr Walters tried to coax him out. In the end he had to get a hook on his collar. He used the pole with the hook on the end that we pull the blinds down with. You should have seen that poor mutt being dragged outside with his tail between his legs.'

'He wasn't rough with it,' defended Lenore, who adored the doctor from a distance. 'He was very gentle.'

'Poor old Rex,' said Eric Maguire, 'he wondered what had hit him. He's never been marched out of anywhere before.' He looked suitably indignant on behalf of his pet.

Andie assured herself that all was well and then motioned the two young nurses to follow her. Outside, glancing from Jessica to Lenore, she said, 'Why didn't one of you call for help the minute Mr Maguire fell over? You only had to press a call button. I told you I'd be in Reba's office. You know the calls light up in there as well as in the nurses' station.'

They looked stunned. 'I never thought of it,' said Lenore, and Jessica's mouth just dropped open.

'I suppose Dr Walters tore a strip off *you*,' she said apologetically.

'He wasn't exactly pleased.'

'Sorry,' said each of the junior nurses in turn. 'It just happened so quickly, we didn't think.'

Andie smiled. 'Well, there's no harm done, but remember that in a crisis nurses never panic, never lose their cool, and always remember what the procedures are. You could be in a life-and-death situation one day, and if you don't think someone might die.'

After visiting time was over, Andie went back to the ward to ask Mr Thompson a few more questions. Then she went to find Cam. He might still be angry with her, but she had to put her theory to him regardless.

He was in his office and called curtly to her to come in. As she entered and he ran his eyes over her slim uniformed figure he could not help seeing her as she had been yesterday at the waterhole, a water nymph in an apple-green swimsuit, her hair drying in the sun, with wisps of it forming a blonde halo about her head as the breeze caught it. What *were* her real feelings about Paul? he wondered, knowing that by even thinking such a thought he was admitting to doubts. Or was he having doubts because he wanted to? Looking at her now, he found himself regretting, as he had last night, that Madeleine had invited herself over after dinner.

'Yes?' he said, using his curt tone, although pretending Andie was just another nurse was scarcely effective.

'Can you spare a few minutes?' Andie asked. 'I want to talk to you about one of the patients.'

Cam motioned her to take a chair. 'What's the problem? Or rather who?'

'Mr Thompson.' He nodded, and looked steadily at her over locked fingers. Andie went on, 'I noticed he has trouble lifting his right arm, especially to shoulder height. It's painful. If I hold it, it's not so bad, and once it's above his head, he's OK.'

Cam looked thoughtful and leaned forward. 'Sounds like frozen shoulder.'

'That's what I think,' she agreed. 'Actually, I was looking it up when all that fracas happened this afternoon, because I was sure there was a connection with diabetes.'

Cam rose and came around his desk to sit on the edge near her. 'You're right, of course, there is.'

Andie rushed on, 'I just wondered, seeing Mr Thompson has been rather accident-prone lately, if it wasn't as a result of the frozen shoulder. He says he's had it for months, but he's not one to complain, so he hasn't asked for any treatment. But if he's stretching and reaching when he's pruning trees, it might be OK in some positions and then give him a sharp jab in others. It can be very painful.'

'I know.'

'Yes. . . Well, is it possible that when he's had a sudden jab, that's when he's jerked a bit, his arm has slipped, and he's cut himself, without realising quite how it happened?'

Cam stroked his chin. 'Very possible.' He smiled at her in admiration. 'Pretty good deduction, Andie. It never occurred to me.'

'Well, unless you'd noticed that his shoulder was giving him trouble, it wouldn't,' she said. 'He doesn't complain, you see, because he's afraid of losing his job. But he shouldn't be allowed to do such dangerous work in that condition.'

'Definitely not,' he agreed. He stood up and paced a few steps away. 'I'd better take a look at him.'

She said anxiously, 'Maybe he could be given some lighter duties for a few weeks until it's better, or sick leave for a couple of months. Is there anyone you could speak to at the council? They might be more sympathetic if they know what the problem is.'

'I'll look into it,' Cam promised. He came back to her, standing very close. 'It was a very pleasant weekend, Andie. I'm glad you came.'

'I'm glad you asked me,' Andie said, hardly daring to meet his eyes. 'It was great. Thanks a lot.'

'You must come up again some time,' he offered.

She smiled. 'Thanks.' But she wouldn't go again, she decided there and then.

'You're a little clever boots!' said Barry, with just the tiniest tinge of resentment behind his smile.

It was a couple of days later and Andie looked up from the blood and other samples she was preparing to send off in the special medical freight box to a pathology laboratory in Adelaide. Barry was watching her intently, and she keenly felt the antagonism below the surface of his good humour.

'That doesn't sound like a compliment,' she said cautiously. Barry had been a little cool towards her lately. She had realised it was probably inevitable since his idea of a friendly relationship was somewhat differ-

ent from hers. Her firm refusal to go to bed with him
was a blow to his ego. Barry was not accustomed to
rebuffs, and in her case he had evidently been confident that perseverance would win the day. It hadn't.

He came closer and slid an arm around her waist.
Andie flinched. When he wasn't propositioning her,
she liked Barry. Why couldn't he realise that seducing
young women was only a temporary ego-booster? And
that he had no need to keep proving himself. She
sighed and moved out of his way.

'I'm busy, Barry. I've got to get these samples
packed.'

He folded his arms across a cripsly laundered pale
blue shirt, which was tucked into pale grey polyester
trousers. His eyes were deceptively ingenuous.

'I was referring to your diagnosis of Dean
Thompson's condition,' he said. 'He's my patient, you
know.'

'Yes, I know.' Andie guessed that his resentment
was because she had voiced her suspicions to Cam, not
him. 'But Cam treated him when he was admitted as a
casualty.'

'It was very clever of you to notice he had frozen
shoulder and suggest that it might be a contributing
factor to his higher than usual incidence of injury.'

She shrugged. 'It seemed an idea worth pursuing.
At least it lessens the risk if he isn't using a dangerous
tool like a power saw. I believe he's going to be
relocated to mowing lawns when he goes back to work,
at least until his shoulder is better.'

Barry's mouth twitched again, with faint resentment.
'Thanks to Dr Walters, I believe. Ethically, of course,
he should have referred the matter to me. His interference makes me look less than competent.'

'Interference? Makes you look incompetent? Oh,
come on, Barry.' Andie packed her last tube into the
container. She gave him a straight look. 'It doesn't

matter, does it? So long as Mr Thompson has less risk of sawing off an arm or a leg.'

Barry's eyes had narrowed as he lounged against the bench. 'You're beautiful, Andie. Does Cam tell you that too?'

She blinked, startled. 'Cam?'

'Did you have a nice weekend at Marshall's Creek?' Barry asked, watching her face.

'I had a very pleasant weekend, thank you.' Andie willed herself not to blush, so as not to give Barry the slightest reason for speculation. 'I've never been to the Flinders Ranges. I had no idea the scenery was so magnificent.'

'It must have been very cosy,' he went on, 'just you and Cam, with the Pattersons away.'

She shot him as disdainful a look as she could muster. 'It wasn't cosy, it was hot! And Fritz was there, of course, and Madeleine Trentham came over on Sunday evening. If you're trying to insinuate something, Barry, don't. It's very bad manners, and so far yours have been impeccable, so don't spoil your image.'

'You mean you spent the whole weekend with Cameron Walters and kept him at arm's length all the time?' Barry mocked. 'You expect me to believe that! You mean he didn't even try to. . .' He grabbed her hard around the waist and pulled her roughly against him, crushing her pelvis against his, as he kissed her with rough passion.

Andie's struggles to release her mouth and escape his clutches were futile, and seemed only to inflame him. It was an impatient rattle of the door handle that broke them apart, to her relief, although she was none too happy when she saw that it was Cam demanding attention. His look was coldly derisive.

'I'm sorry to interrupt,' he drawled sarcastically, 'but the courier's here. Have you finished, Sister Somers?'

He made it sound ambiguous—finished with the packing, or Dr Lester?

Face scarlet, hands and knees trembling, not because of Barry's ardour, but because of Cam's suppressed anger, Andie muttered, 'Yes,' and handed over the locked box of medical test samples. Cam took it from her wordlessly, but his look spoke loudly.

As he left them, she turned angrily on Barry. 'That was a stupid thing to do,' she flung at him. 'I'm on duty! If you want to make a nuisance of yourself, at least do it away from the hospital.'

Barry's smile was unrepentant, in fact blatantly triumphant. 'But it gave Cam something to think about, didn't it? Now he'll think you're two-timing him.'

'He'll think nothing of the sort—he has no reason to. There's nothing whatsoever between Cam and me. No more than between you and me.'

'You should join a cause,' Barry said evenly. 'You're very good at protesting, Andie.'

Andie gritted her teeth and made an effort to keep her temper under control. What difference did it make what Cam thought? That he probably wouldn't believe that she had been an unwilling victim of Barry's ardour was aggravating, however, not because of any personal reason, she told herself, but because she had been caught behaving in what looked like a very unseemly way when she was on duty, and in fact in the middle of performing an important task requiring her whole attention. No doubt Cam would take her to task over it later, or ask Matron to.

CHAPTER EIGHT

THE trouble with night shifts, Andie thought morosely one evening, was that, although they were a substitute when you weren't able to sleep, they still offered too much time for thinking.

At Boobera Hospital the nights were long and uneventful. Andie found her thoughts straying often to Cam and Paul and the invidious position she was in. Paul would never admit to his brother that he had been in the wrong. So what did it matter? It mattered a lot, she discovered, more since Cam had kissed her.

But that meant nothing, she told herself severely. Cam was a normal, virile man who reacted to a half-naked female in a bathing suit in a normal virile way. Just as she had reacted to him. There was no deeper feeling involved than a strong physical attraction that made holding each other and kissing a pleasurable experience. She was determinedly rational about it. She was not even going to begin to think of Cam in any other way. He might be tempted to make love to her, but it would never be more than lust. She hated the word, but it helped to put things in perspective. Cam despised her for, as he believed, walking out on Paul with another man, and for lying to him about it. And anyway, there was Madeleine.

On Sunday night Madeleine Trentham had made it very clear in a number of not very subtle ways that she regarded Cam as her property. Every time he went out to the kitchen to fetch drinks or ice, she contrived to say something pointed to Andie to underline her prior claims. And when Andie left them alone, she heard laughter and intimate murmuring, which ceased the moment she reappeared. Andie almost felt sorry for

Madeleine. Jealousy was a painful emotion. She ought to have been able to say, 'Stop being silly, Madeleine. I don't want him! I'm not the slightest bit interested in him.' But the words had remained unspoken.

At the usual regular intervals, Andie toured the wards and checked that all the patients were sleeping, or if not were comforted with warm drinks and sedatives. An overweight patient with high-blood-pressure problems was snoring loudly when she went round just after midnight. Fortunately he was in a room on his own so was not disturbing anyone else. Very gently, so as not to waken him, Andie rolled him on to his side and plumped up his pillows. He gave a few grunts and settled down to less noisy but heavy breathing.

Andie, and Marion who was on duty with her, settled down too, to a cup of tea and biscuits.

'Mr Parsons really ought to lose weight,' Andie remarked. She grinned. 'I'm glad I'm not Mrs Parsons: he snores dreadfully. I've never heard such peculiar noises!'

Marion suggested, 'Maybe she snores too and drowns him out! I suppose being a publican makes it hard to stay slim. He likes his booze and there's always stacks of food at his elbow. I think she sneaked a couple of pies in for him today—there were foreign crumbs in the bedclothes!'

'But he's supposed to be on a diet,' Andie said.

Marion gestured helplessly with her hands. 'Supposed to be. It we can't get him to stick to it in hospital, and his wife won't co-operate, what chance is there?'

'His blood-pressure's high, and his cholesterol is nine.'

'Well, Cam's trying to treat him, but he can't force patients to look after their bodies, can he?' Marion took the opportunity to add, 'How did you enjoy your weekend at Marshall's Creek?'

'It was great. Cam took me on a flight over the Ranges. I had no idea the scenery was so grand.'

'I reckon he fancies you,' Marion mused teasingly.

Andie forced herself to be casual. 'I have the impression that Dr Walters's only romantic interest is Madeleine Trentham.'

Marion poured more tea. 'Mmm, I don't know. She used him as a crutch when her husband died. After all, he does live next door and is up there as often as he can be. But I don't know that he's as keen as she is.'

'What makes you think that?' Andie tried not to sound too interested.

Marion shrugged. 'They're very different sorts of people. She doesn't really like the outback. She wants to go back to Sydney, so she says, as soon as she can sell Tourmaline, but would he let her drag him back with her?'

'If he loves her. . .'

'*If* he loves her. . .' echoed Marion with emphasis.

Andie glanced at the clock. 'Well, I'd better take another stroll around.' She yawned. 'At least it keeps me awake.'

Marion agreed, and they parted to carry out their separate responsibilities. The hospital was very quiet. Only the hum of the air-conditioning and the distant sound of crickets singing in the grounds disturbed the silence. Even Mr Parsons wasn't snoring, Andie thought with satisfaction as she opened the door to his room. The light from the corridor illuminated the room dimly and she could see the large lump of him in the bed. He was lying on his back again, but not snoring. He was lying very still. There was no sound of breathing at all, no movement of the bedclothes.

Andie hurried to the bedside and clasped the limp wrist that lay outside the bedclothes. 'Mr Parsons!' she said urgently. 'Mr Parsons!' She let go of his wrist and felt desperately for the carotid artery in his neck. Then she turned and ran for help.

Marion came instantly to her aid, and while Andie called Cam the other nurse started mouth-to-mouth resuscitation. Andie joined her to carry out external cardiac massage. Without a word they worked in unison in the attempt to reinflate the man's lungs and start his heart working again. Neither spoke. Each needed her breath and strength for the exhausting work.

In less than five minutes Cam was there, a light jacket pulled on over his pyjamas, his dark hair tousled. The sight of him released a little of Andie's tension. 'Get the defibrillator,' he said grimly to her. 'And hurry! I'll carry on here.' He took over the heart massage with vigour.

Andie raced for the resuscitation trolley, but every nerve in her said it was too late. The patient's colour, the total lack of pulse, the very stillness of him warned her that their efforts might be in vain. She watched helplessly as Cam applied the electrodes, and tried to believe that the convulsive movements induced by the electric shocks would restore the heartbeat. She had seen patients revived when they had seemed to be dead, in the theatre and in the ward, but she knew that all the human effort and all the technology sometimes could not bring back that spark of life. And how long had it been since Mr Parsons' life had ebbed away? How long before she had found him?

Beads of perspiration were standing out on Cam's forehead and the lines between his eyes were deeply etched as he watched the ECG monitor for the vital sign they were all praying for, the blips that would signal that a dead heart was beating again.

It didn't come. Finally Cam said, 'I don't think we can do any more.'

'He's gone,' Marion murmured, almost disbelieving that such a thing could happen. 'We couldn't save him.' She glanced at the other two with accusation in her eyes as though it was their fault, but Andie knew

it was only a reaction. Perhaps her own eyes involuntarily laid blame too. But no one was to blame. A
heart attack could be swift and lethal and too severe
for any chance of revival. Life was a fickle, elusive
thing, sometimes surviving impossible odds, sometimes
being snuffed out as easily as a candle.

A pink dawn was seeping in over the Ranges when
Marion handed Andie a mug of sweet tea. 'Here, you
need something to pep you up.'

Andie smiled wanly. 'Thanks.' She had done everything for Mr Parsons that was necessary. His family
had been, and gone again. But the sadness, the sense
of failure lingered. Soon it would be time for her to go
off duty. She felt utterly drained. She said in anguish,
'If only I'd gone back sooner. . .'

Marion patted her shoulder. 'It wasn't your fault.
You checked at the usual times. You can't be with
them every minute.'

But when someone dies, someone who was in your
care, Andie thought, you always feel responsible. You
always wonder if you could have saved them. A
number on the call board lit up and Marion went to
see what the patient needed. Andie slumped over the
desk, feeling as though she wanted to weep, but too
exhausted even to shed tears.

A hand on her shoulder roused her. It wasn't Marion
this time, but Cam, and now the sight of him in his
maroon pyjamas with a blue blazer over them made
her smile. 'You look slightly ridiculous,' she said.

He smiled down at her. 'Thanks!' He sat down. 'Any
tea left?'

Andie looked in the pot. 'I'll top it up.' She got up
to switch on the kettle, then sat down again.

Cam asked, 'How was he earlier in the evening?'

Her brow puckered. 'All right. I'd looked in about
half an hour before. He was snoring then, so I rolled
him on to his side.'

'He was on his back when you found him later?'

'Yes. I don't know how long—too long, obviously.'
She looked at Cam with anguish. 'If only I'd looked in
again sooner.'

He reached across and covered her hand with his.
'Now don't start blaming yourself. You checked when
you were supposed to. He must have been gone for
some minutes. It might be as well we couldn't revive
him.'

Andie clamped her lips together and moistened
them, biting into her bottom one to stop the surge of
emotion running through her. She knew that brain
damage was a possibility if a person was clinically dead
for too long, that even as short a time as five minutes
could be dangerous.

'If he'd stayed on his side. . .' she sighed.

Cam nodded. 'His heavy snoring does point to the
possibility of sleep apnoea. It was something I wanted
to have investigated, especially in view of the abnor-
mality in his ECG. But he wouldn't go down to
Adelaide for more tests.' He sighed. 'An angiogram
would have revealed how bad he was, and maybe
angioplasty, a bypass, one of the newer techniques
might have saved him. But all we could do, Andie,
was keep him in for a few days and try to bring his
blood-pressure down. We can't force people to do
what we know they should do.'

She looked at him sympathetically. 'You're blaming
yourself too, aren't you? You're wondering if you
should have tried harder to persuade him.'

He squeezed her hand. 'We're both experiencing
fairly normal reactions. But we can only do our jobs
to the very best of our ability, Andie. We're not
miracle-workers and we don't have crystal balls. If we
knew what was going to happen, we'd try harder to
prevent it, but we can't know.'

Andie felt comforted. His hand resting over hers
was warm and reassuring. He had not said a word, she

realised, about finding her in Barry's arms two days ago. No reprimand, nothing.

Cam reached out and tidied a strand of hair off her face. The night's frantic activity had taken its toll of her usually smooth grooming. There were dark smudges under her eyes, and her cheeks were pale. She was almost all in.

'You need to get some sleep,' he told her.

'I will. I'm off all day. I don't suppose you got much last night,' Andie said. The kettle whistled and she filled the teapot.

Cam shrugged. 'That's the way it goes.' He couldn't take his eyes off her. She looked so small and vulnerable, so in need of comfort and protection. He wanted to gather her into his arms and smother that pale, beautiful face with kisses. He wanted. . .so much more . . .but. . . Better to leave her to Barry. His teeth ground inside tight lips as he thought of the other doctor, of Andie in his arms as he'd seen them. Boldly, blatantly, in the hospital. It had incensed him at the time and he'd been ready to tear a strip off her, but when he'd realised that his reasons for wanting to do so were more personal than professional he'd resisted the urge.

Mr Parsons's death cast gloom over the hospital for several days. Everyone knew the jovial publican, of course, and everyone who was able went to the funeral. His son, who had worked with his father, took over, and after a short break away with her sister Sheila Parsons returned to the Boobera Hotel.

For Andie it was a whole new experience. In a big city hospital, which was where she had always worked before, the loss of a patient was deeply felt, but still impersonal. Once the close relatives had been comforted, they disappeared from the scene into their own lives, but here the lives of Boobera people and the

hospital were intertwined. Here the personal involvement was so much greater.

'Sometimes I wish I worked in the city,' Reba said
once, 'where I was completely anonymous and unin-
volved.' She laughed. 'But I know I'd soon be aching
to come back. My roots are here, I'm part of the
scenery.'

'It might be different if you married someone who
wasn't from Boobera,' Andie said.

'Some hopes!' snorted Reba.

Andie speculated whether Reba would leave with
Barry if he ever asked her. She rather thought she
might. Being alone away from familiar surroundings
was one thing; having a loving companion to share
your life with was quite different. She would never
have thought of coming to Australia, she knew, if it
hadn't been for Paul, and many times since their break-
up she had thought of going back to England, but she
hadn't. Her brothers and their families had all gone
abroad too, to America, Canada and the Middle East,
so she no longer had any close family back there, and
even though she'd lost Paul something intangible had
persuaded her to stay.

She was putting down roots in Boobera, she realised
in some surprise, even after only a few weeks there.
What it was about this remote outback town and its
small population, she wasn't sure, but she felt comfortable there. The lack of privacy that had at first irritated
her she had soon taken in her stride. And the friendly
'family' atmosphere at the hospital appealed to her
more than she had thought it would. Working as a
nurse assumed an even more satisfying role.

She was strolling along the main street one Friday
afternoon, on the way back to her car after having
made a few purchases, when she almost collided with
Fritz Weber, who strode out of the hardware store.

'Hello there! My lucky day!' he said, clasping her
arms briefly. 'How are you, Andie?'

'Fine. And you?' His obvious admiration was
flattering.

'Great.'

'What are you doing in town?' It was the first time
she had ever seen Fritz in Boobera.

'A minor emergency. I brought Moira down to go to
the dentist. Their car needed a service, anyway.'

'You drove?'

'Yes. Case of have to, since Cam has the Cessna.
Moira'll go back with him, though.'

'Is Derek with you?' she asked.

'No.' He looked questioningly at her. 'You haven't
met Moira, have you? I'm just about to collect her
from the dentist's and take her to Cam's place. I'll tell
Jean you're coming in for a cup of tea. OK?' He darted
a look at her shopping bags. 'I take it you're on your
way home?'

'Well, yes. . .'

'See you shortly,' said Fritz, giving her arm a
squeeze.

Andie had barely arrived home and stashed her
groceries away when Fritz banged on the door. 'Tea's
up,' he said. As they walked across to the house, he
asked, 'When are you coming up to Marshall's Creek
again?'

She shrugged. 'I don't suppose. . .well, I didn't
expect to make a habit of it.'

He looked at her curiously. 'You surprise me.'

'What do you mean?'

'I thought you and Cam hit it off rather well. You
even had Madeleine biting her nails.'

'Don't be silly,' Andie said crossly.

She was warmly greeted by Jean, and introduced to
Cam's manager's wife. Moira was in her early sixties,
Andie judged, and trim as a teenager in her battle
jacket and jeans. Her face was swollen on one side.

'Excuse my ugly face,' she said. 'I suppose Fritz told you I've been to the dentist.' She looked Andie over with candid blue eyes and her smile seemed to be approving.

'Nice to meet you, Andie. I thought Fritz might have been exaggerating.'

Fritz winked at Andie, who blushed.

He said, 'I was just saying to Andie it's high time she came up to Marshall's Creek again. She looks as though she needs a break, don't you think, Jean?' He turned to Cam's housekeeper, sure of support.

Jean did not disappoint. 'The trouble is they all work too hard at the hospital,' she said. 'There just aren't enough pairs of hands, and when there's a full house the poor girls are worked off their feet.'

'So are the doctors,' Andie hastened to say.

Moira nodded. 'Everyone needs to get away from work. It does Cam the world of good spending weekends at Marshall's Creek.'

'You've been looking very peaky, dear,' said Jean, 'ever since you've had to do night shifts. You don't get enough time off, that's the trouble.'

'I'm off all this weekend,' Andie told her, which proved to be a mistake.

'Then why not come back with us?' offered Moira. She peered at Andie. 'Yes, you do look washed out. You need some mountain air and invigorating bush walks.'

Andie was taken aback. 'Oh, but I couldn't! Cam. . .'

'Cam won't mind,' said Moira confidently. 'What do you say? It won't take you long to pack a bag, will it? Or do you have something special to do this weekend?'

'Well, no. . .not really.' Andie wished she hadn't told the truth. Cam wasn't going to be pleased. Andie was sure he would not want her there again. He would have asked her himself if he had. He had been avoiding her again lately, she was sure. 'But I don't want to impose.'

'We love having people to stay,' Moira assured her.

Andie could see that it would be difficult to argue her way out of it since all three of them were determined she should have a break. To turn the opportunity down flat would seem so ungrateful.

'It's very kind of you,' she said. 'I enjoyed myself very much the last time I was there. It was so relaxing.'

'That's settled, then,' Moira smiled, then winced as her drawn tooth gave a twinge. 'The anaesthetic's wearing off already.'

'I'm off,' said Fritz, getting up. He winked again at Andie. 'See you!'

'A very nice young man,' Moira commented as Fritz left. 'He does a wonderful job.' She slid a glance at Andie. 'And he's very taken with you, if I'm not wrong.'

Andie noticed that Jean frowned slightly as though she did not share Moira's approval of Fritz. Andie said lightly, 'I don't suppose he sees too many young women in his job!'

Moira tried to laugh and winced again. 'He doesn't seem to mind. He's very wrapped up in his field studies.' She wagged a finger at Andie. 'But that doesn't mean he can't appreciate a pretty face when he sees one.'

'Who can't?'

Cam's deep questioning tones reverberated around the room and the three women all turned to look at him. His eyes rested on Andie for a moment before he walked into the room.

'Fritz!' said Moira.

And Jean said, 'Tea, Cam?' She seemed a little withdrawn, Andie thought. She was more reserved than Moira, a different kind of person altogether. He nodded, and Jean scurried off to fetch a cup.

'Fritz has just gone,' Moira told him. 'We were teasing Andie. I'm sure he fancies her!'

'Who wouldn't?' Cam's tone was light, but the glance he bestowed on Andie was faintly scathing.

'She isn't giving anything away,' Moira said, with a smile at Andie. 'But she blushes prettily.'

Jean returned and Cam accepted the cup of tea she poured for him. He perched on the arm of the couch and managed with just a look to make Andie feel even more embarrassed.

'Andie's coming up for the weekend,' Moira breezed on. 'You don't mind, do you, Cam?'

He looked momentarily startled, then said smoothly, 'Of course not. She's welcome any time.' He added, to her, 'I was going to ask you if you'd like to on your next free weekend,' which Andie was sure was a lie. He then made it worse by saying, 'Moira's a notorious matchmaker. You and Fritz had better watch out!'

Moira tried to laugh again, and her face contorted. 'Drat that tooth! Please be serious, everyone.'

'How about a couple of paracetamols?' Cam suggested. 'They'll help. And then I'd like to get going as soon as possible.' He glanced at Andie again. 'How long will it take you to pack?'

Andie was all churned up, wondering how she'd managed to land herself in such an invidious position. 'I don't want to hold you up,' she said hastily. 'Perhaps another time. . .'

She thought Cam looked relieved, but extricating herself was not so easy. Moira was quite sure they could wait half an hour. Having extended the invitation, she was evidently unwilling to look as though she regretted it.

So, a short time later, having hurriedly showered and changed and thrown a few clothes into a holdall, she rejoined them.

The flight to Marshall's Creek, almost directly into the sunset, was spectacular, and just to see the Ranges on fire with the afterglow was enough to make Andie glad she had come. It was almost dark on the ground when they arrived, and there was a distinct chill in the air as they alighted from the aircraft. Instead of Fritz to meet them this time, it was Derek Patterson, in the Toyota truck.

'Hi there, pleased to meet you,' he greeted Andie. He was a big man, jovial like his wife, and he gripped her hand hard.

Once again she found herself crammed in the cabin of the Toyota, this time between Fritz and Moira, while Cam travelled in the back. It was an eerie journey, with the headlights flashing across the bush like searchlights, as Derek negotiated the twisting track, and sometimes reflecting off the eyes of nocturnal creatures. Twice Derek braked suddenly as a large kangaroo froze in front of them before bounding off into the bush.

Moira showed her to the same room as she'd slept in the last time and threw her some clean linen to make up the bed. 'While I get the dinner,' she said.

'Can I help?' asked Andie.

'I expect so,' Moira said cheerfully. 'Come out to the kitchen when you're ready and Cam'll give you a drink.'

Andie tried not to feel awkward, but she wished she hadn't come. Cam didn't want her here. She didn't want to be here. But bush hospitality was not something you threw back in a person's face, and Moira had only meant to be kind. Surely her motive hadn't been matchmaking? Andie thought about Fritz and sighed wearily. Was he going to be another complication in her life? She must make sure he hadn't got any wrong ideas.

Uneasily she strolled along to the kitchen, to find a heated argument going on. Moira had collapsed in a chair and Cam was bending over her with a stethoscope. Derek was standing by looking worried.

'What's wrong?' At the sound of Andie's voice, Cam glanced up at her.

'Nothing!' said Moira, but without her previous ebullience. 'These men are just fussing.'

Cam said, 'She blacked out. We're trying to get her to go to bed.'

'I've got to get dinner,' Moira insisted.

He gave Andie a look of appeal, and she said at once, 'Don't worry about that—I'll get the dinner. Just tell me what we're having.'

'Pizza,' murmured Moira resignedly now. 'And salad. You'll find several pizzas in the freezer. And I was going to make a fresh fruit salad.'

'That sounds easy,' said Andie. She glanced at Cam, then back at Moira. 'Shall I help you get undressed?'

Moira pressed her hand. 'What a good thing you came, Andie.' She allowed Cam and her husband to help her along to her bedroom, and seemed grateful for Andie's help to undress. 'I never faint,' she said. 'I hope there's nothing wrong with me.'

'It was probably a reaction to having the wisdom tooth out,' Andie told her, 'and then getting shaken up in the truck. I expect you'll be fine in the morning.'

There was a knock and Cam came in. 'What you need, Moira, is a good night's sleep. You overdo things, you know.'

She pulled a face at him. A few minutes later, back in the kitchen, Andie said, 'She's a ball of energy, isn't she? The kind who never knows when to stop.'

Both Cam and Derek agreed. Derek said anxiously, 'She's never fainted before. It's not a sign of something serious, is it, Cam?'

Cam shook his head. 'No, I'm sure it's not. I think it was just the stress of having the tooth out, a reaction to the anaesthetic, maybe, and the pain when it wore off. I'll have her in for tests if I think there's any need.'

'I was afraid it might have been a stroke,' Derek ventured worriedly.

'At her age it could have been. A very minor one, though. They can even happen sometimes without the person realising it. But there's no reason to think it's a warning sign, or that she'll have another.'

As she listened to the men talking, Andie prepared dinner and presently served it in the dining-room. Moira was fast asleep, so she did not wake her, and Cam said it was better to just let her rest.

Andie wished she could sleep as soundly. She lay awake that night wondering what on earth she was doing there, and longing for the weekend to be over. This time it was not going to be so relaxing.

At breakfast she was faced with a dilemma. Fritz said, 'I'm going out to the Wakawinya caves to look for bats today, Cam, and I reckon there might be another colony of yellow-footed rock wallabies over there.' He included Andie in his glance and went on, 'You two want to come?'

Cam said, 'Sorry, I can't. I've got to go over to Tourmaline. Madeleine rang just a few minutes ago. One of her staff's down with a rather severe flu, by the sound of it. If it's pneumonia we'll have to hospitalise her.'

Fritz said in a disappointed tone, 'I suppose you'll need Andie.'

Cam shook his head. 'No, I don't think there's any need for you to come, Andie, unless you want to, of course. You're off duty. You ought to be relaxing.'

He didn't want her with him, Andie knew. He was going to see Madeleine, so he wouldn't want her tagging along. She didn't really want to go out with Fritz, but she could hardly say so. Again she was trapped.

'Well, if you're sure you won't need me,' she said.

He gave her an odd look. 'No, you go off with Fritz and enjoy yourself. That's what you came for, wasn't it?'

Andie did not answer. She didn't like his tone at all.

So she went with Fritz, and although she hadn't expected to she enjoyed herself. Her fears that Fritz might be another fast mover like Barry proved to be unfounded. They talked, laughed, and enjoyed each other's company, and although they didn't spot any wallabies they did find bats, and Andie also learned a great deal about the fauna of the Flinders Ranges. If Fritz often gave her admiring looks, he did not follow them up. Andie gradually relaxed.

When they got back to the homestead, she thanked him. 'I had a great day,' she said. 'Thanks for taking me.'

'It was a pleasure,' said Fritz. 'If you ever get tired of nursing, I could do with an assistant!'

Andie put her trail-bike away in the shed and strolled over to the homestead, humming happily. The weekend was not turning out so badly after all. She wondered if Cam was back yet, or would he spend this evening with Madeleine?

'You sound pleased with life. Fritz gave you a good day, I presume.'

The voice came out of the shadows on the veranda, and Andie broke off her humming. Cam was back and seemed in a less than amiable mood. She told him briefly about her day, then asked, 'How was the patient?'

'Just a bad bout of flu. Unfortunately they'll probably all go down with it. They haven't got any visitors at the moment, but there's a party arriving next weekend and then they're busy for several weeks.'

Cam accompanied Andie into the house. Moira was back on deck, complaining that it had all been a fuss about nothing, but grateful to Andie for helping out. Over dinner the conversation again came around to Tourmaline.

'Madeleine must be pleased that Phil Branson's going to take the place off her hands,' said Moira. 'I suppose she'll go back to Sydney as soon as it's settled.'

Andie wondered if that was the reason for Cam's gloomy mood. What would Madeleine do if he asked her to marry him? she wondered. Would she stay, or would he have to go where she wanted? She seemed keen on the sanctuary, but she had admitted to finding Tourmaline rather remote. If she went back to Sydney, and Cam followed, he wouldn't be able to come to Marshall's Creek so often.

After dinner Fritz showed some films of wildlife, and it was midnight when Andie got to bed. She was tired enough to sleep despite her thoughts and dropped into a deep sleep almost at once, but woke again only an hour later, disturbed by dreams that floated out of her grasp, except for a lingering image of Cam receding in the distance while she desperately tried to follow because she was sure he was in danger.

She had been awake for ten minutes or so when a terrifying scream from outside made her leap out of bed. 'God! What was *that*?' she breathed, rushing to the window. She could see nothing in the blackness, but the echo of the scream made her shudder. It hadn't sounded human. An animal in distress? Yes, that must have been what it was. Perhaps a wallaby which had been shot and was running wildly in its agony. What kind of sound did a wallaby make? Andie had no idea.

Unable to just forget it, she slid her feet into thongs and felt her way on tiptoe along the passage to the kitchen, where she remembered seeing a torch. She grabbed it and quietly let herself out the back door. She felt a little foolish now. How was she ever going to find whatever had made that noise in the dark bush? But having got this far, she shone the torch around in the area near her bedroom window. There was nothing. Whatever it had been was proably far away by now, she realised a little sheepishly.

She was about to go back to bed when a shadow loomed up beside her, making her gasp aloud.

'It's all right, it's me,' Fritz's voice reassured her. 'I saw the light. What are you doing?'

Andie clasped his arm. 'Oh, Fritz! You gave me a fright.'

'What on earth are you doing wandering around at this hour?' he demanded.

'I heard a scream, like something in agony. I thought there must be some animal, hurt. . .' She countered with, 'What are *you* doing?'

'I've been studying some possums that use nesting boxes at the back of my cabin. I'm trying to track them at night to check on their feeding habits.'

'You must have heard the scream,' she said.

'I didn't. Sure you didn't dream it?'

'I was awake.' Or had she dropped off without realising it, back into that dream?

Fritz patted her shoulder. 'It could have been a possum, or maybe a dingo caught a rabbit. The bush is full of strange sounds. It might have been further away that you thought—sounds carry at night.'

Andie felt foolish. 'I'd better go back to bed.'

As she was now near the front of the house, she walked up to the veranda knowing that the front door would be open and it was closer to her bedroom. She had almost reached the steps when a strong beam of light dazzled her eyes.

'What the hell's going on?' Cam startled her as much as Fritz had.

'It's only me,' she said weakly, feeling more of a fool than ever. Everyone was going to be on the scene if there was any more noise.

Cam angled the beam away from her as she mounted the veranda steps, explaining in a whisper about the scream. He looked down at her sceptically. 'And Fritz just happened to hear the scream too? It looked more as though he was either walking you home or just leaving. . .'

Andie was stunned. 'How dare you? That's a grossly insulting remark, and I think you should apologise.'

She started to walk past him, but he caught her upper arm and turned her to face him. 'Let me go!' Andie said, trembling. 'You're hurting me.'

Cam released her, but as she moved to go inside he suddenly dropped the torch and dragged her back into his arms. His mouth had made unerring contact with hers before she could draw breath, and as his arms enfolded her she almost felt her ribs crack. A wave of emotion swamped her as she felt herself melt in his arms.

He was only wearing pyjama shorts and despite the coolness of the night the heat of his body was searing through the thin cotton of her nightdress. Andie's torch fell from her fingers as the urge to cling to him overwhelmed her. Her hands slid across his bare back, along his spine, pulling him closer, as she realised that she wanted this man more than anyone she had known. She wanted him, needed him, *loved* him. . .

But he would never love her. She had long since forgiven him, but for him forgiveness would not be enough; he would never trust her, and without trust there could not be lasting love. Her lips opened against his, powerless to resist, and she let herself exult in a fresh wave of passion, happy to drown in the ecstasy of the moment.

'Cam. . .' she whispered, when he moved his lips from hers to kiss her neck and shoulders, the hollow of her throat, the swell of her breasts. He pushed the nightdress off her shoulder, then stopped and looked into her face.

'Why the hell are we standing out here?'

He scooped her up in his arms and carried her into her bedroom. He was appalled at himself, but beyond reason now. He wanted her more than he had ever wanted a woman. He began to lift her nightdress, his hands lightly discovering the smooth shapeliness of her

thighs and waist, the curve of her breasts, the very feel
of her skin maddening his desire.

'Oh, God, you're beautiful!' he whispered, bending
to touch his lips to her nipples.

Andie heard a scream like the scream she'd heard
before, only this time it was in her head. 'No!' It came
out softly, desperately. If she let this happen, she
would never be able to erase it. It would be seared on
to her memory forever. Cam would be. . .

'No, Cam, please. . .' she whispered.

He came to his senses as though someone had
doused him with cold water. What sort of madness was
this? What sort of madman was he?

'I'm sorry,' he said, his voice still husky with desire.
'I just made a fool of myself, didn't I? Forcing myself
on you like that.' He pushed her away. 'I guess I must
have got carried away by the—er—circumstances.'

Andie stood stunned as he backed away and left the
room. Then she flung herself down on the bed and
buried her face in the cool pillow, her shoulders
shaking with a desperate silent sobbing.

CHAPTER NINE

AT BREAKFAST next morning, Andie caught Cam looking broodingly at her once or twice. It was an unbearable situation. She was achingly aware of the intensity of emotion their midnight encounter had unleashed in each of them, but more catastrophic was the realisation that she loved this man. The certainty that he would never love her, and probably regarded her passionate responses to him as merely physical and temporary, as his own were, was a bitter irony.

The whole of Sunday stretched ahead interminably. Andie supposed Cam would return to Boobera in the early hours of Monday as he usually did, which meant another long night at Marshall's Creek. It served her right, she thought. She should never have come. She had let herself be persuaded too easily, but only now was she willing to admit that part of it had been wanting to spend the weekend with Cam again. What a fool she was! If he'd wanted her to come, he would have asked her himself.

After breakfast Cam disappeared with Derek. There were the accounts to go over, he apologised, and discussions they must have about the maintenance of fences and walking tracks. Andie gathered from their conversation at breakfast that there were a couple of scientific groups who wanted to send teams to conduct surveys on the property. This was the only kind of intrusion Cam allowed. He was not interested in developing the property for holidaymakers as the Trenthams had done at Tourmaline.

'Perhaps Fritz can amuse you again today,' Cam said pointedly, his mouth twisting cynically.

The barb hurt, and Andie tried not to mind. 'I don't

want to bother anyone,' she said. 'I'll be able to amuse myself quite well, thanks.'

She helped Moira wash up. Moira was back to normal and still disgusted with herself.

'Such a fuss over having a tooth out!' she said self-disparagingly.

'Wisdom teeth aren't funny,' Andie consoled. 'Plenty of people have to go to hospital for a day or two to have them out. And Cam was naturally a bit worried when you blacked out.'

'He thinks it might have been a stroke, doesn't he?' Moira said, 'even though I haven't any side-effects.' Her glance invited Andie to disagree with the idea.

Andie couldn't. 'If it was, it was very slight,' she said. 'The only way to know would be to have an EEG. It wouldn't be a bad idea, you know, just to check up. I know Cam would like you to.'

Moira snorted, 'Such a fuss!' but Andie sensed that she was more worried than she was showing and needed reassuring.

Andie said, 'A lot of people are afraid to have tests in case something unpleasant comes to light, but that's a very negative approach. If you know what's wrong, the chances are it can be treated and save further problems. If you get a clean sheet then you can stop worrying.'

Moira pulled the plug out of the sink. 'Yes, of course you're right.' She sighed resignedly. 'I'll do whatever Cam says. Now, what would you like to do today? Or are you going somewhere with Fritz again?'

Andie finished wiping the cutlery and hung up the tea-towel. She wished Moira weren't so keen to push her into Fritz's company. 'I think I'll just relax,' she said. 'I might take a walk, explore a little, but nothing too strenuous. Trail-bike riding is quite tiring, I find.'

'Well, make yourself at home,' Moira said. 'If you feel like a cup of coffee or a cool drink any time, just help yourself. If you're hungry, the cake tins are there to be raided!'

'Can I help at all?' Andie asked.

Moira was adamant. 'No—you came up for a break. Just take it easy. You nurses worry too much about everyone else's health and not enough about your own. I want to see those dark smudges disappear from under your eyes.'

To be left to her own devices was precisely what Andie needed. She sat on the veranda for a while, then, feeling restless, decided to go for a walk. She was about to go in to change into walking shoes when Fritz appeared, carrying a large sacking bundle in his arms. His expression was furious.

'What's the matter?' Andie ran to meet him. 'What's that? Oh—a kangaroo.' She could just see the large ears, wide brown eyes and soft snout of the animal.

'Wallaby,' said Fritz tightly, and let fly a torrent of invective against 'macho idiots with guns who get their kicks taking pot-shots at anything that moves'.

'Is it badly hurt?' Andie asked.

'They got her in the leg,' said Fritz. 'Where's Cam?'

'With Derek in the house.'

Fritz marched towards the door, and Andie hurried to open it for him. Cam and Derek were coming along the passage. Cam guessed at once what was wrong. He looked at the frightened animal in the sack and swore as vehemently as Fritz, then glanced apologetically at Andie. 'Sorry. . .' He turned back to Fritz. 'What's the damage?'

'She was shot in the hind leg. She has a joey in the pouch.'

Cam frowned. 'I'll see what I can do. Bring her out the back.' He gave Andie a quirky look. 'I'm not a vet, but I've learned a fair bit about fixing wildlife since I've been here. Want to help?'

Andie abandoned all idea of a walk. 'Yes. Yes, of

course.' She was eager to help, but nervous. She had never encountered an injured animal before.

In a closed-off section of the back veranda, which she guessed was kept for such emergencies, the injured wallaby was laid on a table and the sacking removed from its hindquarters. The sacking was bloody, and the matted fur and blood on the animal's thigh indicated where the shot had penetrated. The terrified wallaby kicked wildly, desperate to get away, but Fritz held it firmly and kept the sack loosely over its head to minimise its struggling.

'Looks like the shot's still in there,' said Cam, examining the leg. 'If the bone isn't shattered, we might be able to save her.'

'Oh, look, there's the joey!' exclaimed Andie as the baby tried to scramble out of his mother's pouch.

'Get a hold of him, Andie,' Cam instructed. 'No, not with your bare hands, he might scratch and kick. Grab one of those old towels in the basket and wrap it round him firmly. Moira will take care of him.'

Andie grabbed a towel and swiftly captured the joey in it, holding the struggling animal gingerly because she was afraid of hurting it. Moira, alerted to the situation by Derek, came in.

'I think Joey had better be looked after separately for the time being,' Cam said. 'With a bit of luck he might not lose his mum.'

Moira took the tiny animal from Andie, then said, 'You're going to help Cam? Good. You'll find an apron in the cupboard. I'll settle this little fellow down in the kitchen.'

Andie looked at Cam. 'What do you want me to do?'

'Help me remove shotgun pellets from the leg.' His face relaxed from the brooding expression of earlier in the morning. He opened a cupboard and showed her an aray of surgical instruments and medications.

'You'd better sterilise these.' He dropped the instruments he would need into a stainless-steel kidney dish.

Andie raced off to the kitchen and found that Moira, anticipating the need, had already set a saucepan of water to boil. She had also settled the joey, wrapped in an old cardigan, in a high-sided box.

'So he hardly knows he isn't in the pouch,' she explained. 'We'll just keep him quiet for a bit, then I'll mix him up some formula.' She smiled at Andie's look. 'Yes, we have a special baby formula for joeys.'

'He wasn't hurt?'

'No, luckily.'

For Andie, the next hour was an illuminating experience. At first it seemed very strange to be assisting an operation on a patient with a furry body, claws and a long tail, but after a few minutes, like Cam, her only concern was to see the shotgun pellets removed and the wound stitched.

Cam had anaesthetised the animal, which lay immobile on the table, and shaved off a patch of fur around the wound. Fritz stood by while they worked in case he was needed. Removing the pellets was not easy, and took some time.

'No bone damage,' Cam announced at last, when his probing of the wound satisfied him of that. 'She's lucky.' He glanced at Andie. 'Well, I think we've got it all. There's a bit of damage to the muscle, but that should heal all right. We'll give her a week or so's convalescence in the compound and then let her go. Now, sutures, if you please, Andie.'

He was as thorough and gentle with the wallaby, Andie noticed, as with any human patient.

'You did a great job,' she said afterwards, and dared to joke, 'You ought to have been a vet, Cam.'

He actually laughed, and as their eyes met Andie felt that their good relationship had been partially restored at least by this unorthodox shared medical experience. Last night was just something else to put

out of her mind, as Cam had no doubt already put it
out of his. The only problem was that, from her
standpoint, their relationship had changed. She could
never regard him as just a professional colleague ever
again.

'Thanks for your help, Andie,' he said, adding
deadpan, 'You'd have made a great veterinary nurse.'

She grinned. '*Touché*!'

Fritz said, 'If you don't need me, Cam, I'll go and
check the compound fence—we haven't had to use it
for a while. I'll put fresh bedding in the shed, and
stack some grasses for Joey's mum. Shall I bed her
down out there straight away?'

'Sure,' Cam answered. 'She'll be a bit groggy when
she comes round, but by tonight she ought to be
looking lively again. She'll be less stressed in the
compound than here. Keep her in until I come up
again, Fritz, and watch her to make sure she doesn't
get at the wound and open it.'

When Fritz had gone, and Andie was preparing to
wash and replace the equipment they had used, Cam
checked the still unconscious wallaby, then said, 'I'm
going back tonight instead of tomorrow morning,
Andie. OK with you?'

She lifted her eyes, and his dark gaze sent a flurry of
shivers down her spine. 'Fine.' She didn't enquire why,
and he didn't offer any explanation.

So the day which Andie had expected to be intermi-
nable did, in the end, fly by. The operation on the
wounded wallaby had occupied the best part of the
morning, and after lunch Andie found herself helping
Moira with the joey. Sitting in a rocking chair in a
corner of the kitchen, with the small furry animal
wrapped in a cardigan in her lap while she gave it a
bottle, just like any human baby, Andie felt strangely
content. And as she gazed down at the small, defence-
less creature on her lap, its tiny forepaws clutching the
bottle as it sucked, just like a human baby, she closed

her eyes and her mind drifted into a daydream. Instead
of a baby wallaby in her lap there was a human baby
. . .hers. For the first time in her life she thought how
wonderful it would be to have a baby, with dark hair
and dark eyes. . .like Cam's. . .

This crazy thought which had slipped so treacher-
ously into her mind made her eyes flick open, and to
her horror she saw that she was being watched. Moira
had gone out, and Cam was lounging in the doorway,
a reflective expression on his face. For one terrible
moment Andie thought he must know her thoughts,
but of course that was impossible—unless she had
been thinking aloud. . . Andie felt she would die of
mortification if that were so. But Cam gave no sign
that she had been.

'You're looking very maternal,' was all he said,
coming over to tickle the joey behind its ears.

His nearness was almost too much for Andie. She
said shakily, 'This might be the first joey I've ever
bottle-fed, but I'm quite used to feeding human babies.
I've worked on labour wards and children's.' She found
herself staring fascinated at the tiny hairs on the back
of his hands as his fingers moved rhythmically on the
joey's head. His hands were strong but gentle, and she
wished he were touching her. . .

Cam did not comment. He just stood there with her
until the bottle was empty. Andie wiped a splash off
the joey's velvety black nose. Replete now, the little
animal began to doze.

'I'd better put him back in the box,' said Andie.

Cam helped her out of the chair and together they
made the joey comfortable again in its pouch-like
wrappings.

'Poor little thing,' Andie murmured. 'I hope his
mother will be all right.'

'I'm confident she will be,' Cam assured her.

Andie pushed the box into the corner where Joey
would not be disturbed, but Moira could keep an eye

on him, and stood up. 'But she'll be at risk again as soon as you let her go,' she said. 'Isn't there some way to stop people shooting these beautiful creatures?'

Cam shook his head. 'It's not easy to patrol rugged country like this. We can put up all the notices we like saying it's a sanctuary, but that doesn't stop some yahoos trespassing. Fritz does his best, but he can't be everywhere at once. I've been thinking of putting on another ranger, maybe zoology students who could come part-time and do practical studies as well.'

'That sounds a good idea,' Andie approved.

Moira returned and clucked over the joey, while beaming at Andie for her successful feeding of the baby. 'I can see you're an expert,' she laughed. She turned to Cam. 'We'll have an early dinner, so you can leave while there's still plenty of daylight.'

Andie felt uneasy about the flight back to Boobera. Would Cam say anything about last night? She hoped not. She tried to make a mental list of things to talk about so that there wouldn't be any awkwardness. She would talk about the patients at Boobera Hospital, she thought, ask him medical questions, and never let the conversation lapse. That way she might be able to keep her emotions under control. It wasn't as though the ordeal would be long; the actual flight took less than an hour.

In the event, Andie had no problems. She ended up convinced that Cam had made a mental list of topics too, in order to dispel any tension between them. And he evidently had no intention of alluding to anything that had occurred between them at Marshall's Creek. After the first ten minutes in the air, Andie relaxed, and almost before she knew it the Cessna was touching down at Boobera airfield.

Cam's Range Rover was where he had left it on Friday. He carried Andie's holdall and his own bag to it, while she lugged a carton of culinary offerings from

Moira, some for her and some to be handed over to Jean.

Cam said, 'Jean will sniff, of course. With them it's almost a continuous baking competition. Each tries to outdo the other. We men reap the benefit, of course.'

Andie laughed. It was almost relaxed between them now. This was how she must try and keep things, she thought, on this nice even keel, with no emotional involvement. In Cam's eyes she would always have personal shortcomings, but they could still be friends on a certain level at least. If she could have that much of him, it would be better than nothing at all.

As they drove home from the airfield, she thanked him formally for the weekend.

'It was a whole new experience for me,' she said unthinkingly.

'Was it?' Cam's eyes flashed her a look that made her blush.

'I meant scrubbing for a vet!' Andie managed to say lightly.

'Of course,' he answered, and that was as close as they came to mentioning personal matters. 'Are you on duty tomorrow morning?' he asked.

'Yes. And I'm hoping not to have to do double shifts this week.'

Cam swung the Range Rover through the always open front gates of the driveway to his house. 'Hello!' he exclaimed in some surprise. 'Looks like we've got a visitor.'

Andie saw the blue Volvo parked next to her car. 'It's a Victorian number-plate,' she observed, as she started to get out of the Range Rover. 'Will you take the goodies in to Jean or shall I?'

'Andie!' Cam's voice was sharply detaining.

'Yes, what is it?' She paused questioningly, puzzled by the flicker of unease crossing his face. He was looking past her towards the house.

'Andie!' This time it wasn't Cam calling her name.

Andie whipped round in shock to see Paul coming across the gravel towards them. But Cam had said he never came here, and he didn't know she was here. Paul was the last person she had expected to see, the person she least wanted to see.

'Paul. . .' Her mouth was dry, her throat constricting, and she had to fight an overwhelming desire to take to her heels and run.

Cam got out of the Range Rover. Andie glanced at him, then back at Paul. Standing between them as they looked at each other, she felt like a victim caught in crossfire.

'What are you doing here, Paul?' Cam asked in a calm voice.

Paul smiled, the brilliant white smile that gave a sensuous tilt to his mouth and narrowed his eyes so they seemed to smoulder—a heart-melting smile, Andie remembered, one that had once curled her toes and turned her insides into a frenzy. But not any more. For her now Paul had no more charm than the Range Rover. Whatever Paul had done to her, Cam could do a hundred times more devastatingly.

He was looking at her, eagerly, confidently. 'I've come to see Andie,' he said in a coaxing tone, and moving closer. 'It's time we had a little heart-to-heart talk. We have a few misunderstandings to clear up.'

Andie was dumbstruck. She could not take in what was happening. Paul was here. Paul wanted to talk to her. He was still angling for a reconciliation. She wasn't sure she could cope. It was too unexpected.

'How did you know I was here?' she asked numbly, directing an accusing glance at Cam.

'Jean told me.'

'Jean?'

He laughed softly. 'Yes. She didn't know she was letting the cat out of the bag, of course. I phoned on Friday night and we chatted for a bit. She told me Cam was at Marshall's Creek and that the nurse who lived in the annexe had gone too. I could scarcely believe it when she told me your name. How did you know Cam was up here? And why come here anyway? It's the last place I'd have expected you to hide yourself away.'

Andie looked in desperation at Cam, who was giving her a puzzled look. Surely he didn't think. . . But he'd had his suspicions before that it had all been planned. Andie closed her eyes. It was all so complicated. She didn't know what to say first. She opened them again. Cam was looking at her with that old expression of disdain, suggesting he did suspect her of more lies and deception now.

Cam dragged his eyes away from her. He was pleased to see his brother, but apprehensive. 'Why did you phone me, Paul?' he asked. 'Presumably you want something.'

Smiling as though there was no estrangement, Paul snapped his fingers. 'A little business deal I thought you might be interested in,' he said airily.

'Where did you get the Volvo?' asked Cam, eyes narrowing.

Paul waved a hand at the expensive car. 'It's not mine, I borrowed it from my partner. I can only afford an old bomb.' His eyes stopped smiling and accused his brother.

'So what's the business deal?' Cam demanded.

'I'll tell you later,' Paul said. 'I want to talk to Andie first. I was so surprised to hear that she was here, I just had to come up right away.' He wagged a finger at her. 'It was very uncivil of you, darling, to rush off without leaving a forwarding address.'

Andie was still rooted to the ground. Cam finally said decisively, 'Well, if you two want to talk privately, don't mind me.' He grabbed the carton of produce off the back seat of the Range Rover, dumped the top package in Paul's arms, saying, 'That's for Andie,' tucked the box under his arm and with his bag in the other hand strode into the house.

Andie looked at Paul. She might as well get it over with, she thought dismally.

'Paul, will you please get this clear?' Andie said for the umpteenth time. 'I do not want to come back to you. It's no use your trying to persuade me.'

'Andie, you're not even trying to see my point of view,' Paul complained. They were facing each other across the kitchen table and there were two empty beer bottles at his elbow, a pot of tea beside Andie.

'So far as I'm concerned you don't have one,' she said caustically. 'You walked out on me, Paul. You got another woman pregnant. You lied to Cam. I'm beginning to think you only ever wanted me anyway as a passport to getting your inheritance early. That's what you're after even now, isn't it? Well, it won't work. It's finished between us. It was over a long time ago.'

He slid his hand across the table and grasped hers before she could snatch it away. He lifted it to his lips. 'Andie, my love, I know you have a lot to hate me for, but can't we try and make a go of it? I'm truly sorry for the way I treated you. I behaved abominably—I make no excuses. I was a louse. Everything you said— I admit it. But I'm sorry. . .' He smiled the little-boy smile that had once turned her heart over but now only hardened it. 'Give me another chance, Andie. Please. . . I love you. . .'

'You don't,' she said curtly. 'You don't love anyone except yourself, Paul. You think you can break all the rules, hurt and humiliate a person, and then when it suits you apologise and expect them to accept you back with open arms. It's too late, Paul. I'm not in love with you any more.' The reason, she realised, was not just Cam. 'I've grown out of you,' she finished.

His eyes narrowed and his mouth hardened. 'Is there someone else?' he demanded.

Andie swallowed hard, threatened by a betraying rush of emotion. If she said no, he would persist, if she said yes, he would try to find out who. 'That's none of your business,' she said.

'Oh, yes, it is. When my wife. . .'

Andie dragged her hand away. 'I am not your wife! We're divorced, Paul.'

His mouth turned down. 'Oh, yes, I tend to forget. I still think of you as my wife.' His eyes were tender, sensuous, and full of guile, but Andie knew it for an act now. 'You never used to be hard like this. Remember when we first met in London, the fabulous times we had? You were very loving then.' He sighed. 'I never met anyone so loving.'

'You killed my love,' Andie told him, feeling a deep pang of regret. It could have been so good, it could have been wonderful if that first fine careless rapture had endured. Momentarily, she let his words take her back, and allow her to feel as she had five years ago with him. But the feeling was fleeting, a memory that could no longer be recaptured. The excitement, the romance, the bliss of emotional discovery that had seemed so perfect at the time, she now saw to have been superficial. In five years she had changed, grown, matured, and she had met Cam again. What she felt for Cam was so different, so much deeper and meaningful—or would be if only he felt the same and they could share it. If he could believe in her, would that make a difference? Andie trembled at the thought that it might. And Paul was the only person who could make Cam believe in her.

He was looking at her closely. Suspiciously. 'So Jean was right, there is something between you and my brother. Dear old soul that she is, she hopes wedding bells will come of it. I rather dashed her hopes, I'm afraid, when I told her you were married to me. She didn't know. Cam doesn't mention me often, I gather. Black sheep of the family.' He laughed harshly, and the glitter came into his eyes that Andie recalled so well, the glitter of frustration because he was being thwarted. It was the side of him that in the first flush of romance she had not let herself see.

'There's nothng between Cam and me,' she told him.

Paul's smile was sly. 'I told Jean I thought it unlikely, since you always hated each other's guts. But who knows. . .?' He inclined his head and gave her a mocking look. 'Love and hate. . .'

'Cam despises me,' Andie said bitterly. 'He believes your version of our marriage break-up, not mine. You told him I left you. You cried on his shoulder and told him lies about me, and because you're his brother he believed you.'

He looked smug. 'Blood's always thicker than water.' He eyed her reflectively. 'How would you like me to tell him the truth?'

Andie regarded him warily. 'I think you owe it to me.'

He poured another glass of beer. His face was flushed. He began to look pleased with himself. 'If I tell Cam the truth, will you come back to me? He can't not approve of you now.'

Andie half rose, and sank back again. 'No. . . Paul, that's despicable.'

He pushed his chair back and it toppled over. He was drunk, she realised. He'd probably had a few drinks before they'd arrived back. He staggered a little and leaned on the edge of the table near her. He swallowed most of the beer in his glass.

'You're drunk,' Andie said with distaste. 'I think you'd better go. We have nothing more to say to each other. If you have any decency, Paul, you'll tell Cam the truth and apologise to him, not me.'

He leered at her. 'Andie—darling—don't be a

spoilsport. If I tell Cam the truth, he'll have to approve of us getting married again. Jean said he thinks very highly of you. Now he *knows* you, now he knows you're not just a money-grubbing little gold-digger. . .'

'Paul, I'm not going to marry you just so you can get your hands on your grandfather's money. That wasn't why I married you in the first place, although I did think it was unfair that Cam could inherit and you couldn't. I've changed my mind since. Your grandfather was very sensible to tie up your share like that. He knew you were irresponsible. And it seems you still are, to make a proposal like that to me.'

Her ex-husband glowered, and his eyes were unfocused. 'For God's sake, Andie,' he whimpered, 'give me a break! I've got the chance of a lifetime, an investment opportunity that'll set us up for good. All I need is the capital.'

Andie knew she had no reason to feel guilty, but she did—for not wanting to help him. She did want to help him, but not this way. Once she had loved this man, once she had been a loyal wife, but the well of her feelings had dried up. When he had first come back into her life and tried to get her back, she had been confused and uncertain. She had come to Boobera to sort out that confusion, and until this weekend she had not been completely sure that she had. Now she was sure.

'Please go, Paul,' she said firmly. 'I'm tired and I want to go to bed.'

He slid along the table edge to her. 'So do I, Andie, so do I,' he breathed huskily.

Andie leapt up. 'Don't you dare! Don't you dare touch me!'

He lunged towards her, caught her before she could flee and crushed her tightly against him. 'Why not, my sweet? There was a time when. . .'

'Let me go!' Andie sobbed. 'I don't want you. Let me go!'

His face was buried against her neck, which he began to kiss moistly. His hands groped wildly, trying to remove her clothing, as he pushed her towards the door to the passage leading to her bedroom. He wasn't so drunk he didn't know what he was doing. This was to be his final bid to persuade her. He probably believed she would not be able to resist him. So many of their early quarrels had ended in bed that he was no doubt confident of his ability to win her over once more.

Andie struggled wildly, but, despite his unsteadiness, he was strong. As they approached her bedroom, Andie panicked. The door was open, and her strength was ebbing. She made one last effort to fling him off, and when that failed, she deliberately tripped and fell, bringing him down with her. The shock made him release her, and she scrambled up and fled into her bedroom, shooting the bolt on the inside, thankful that there was one.

Pale and shaking, she leaned on the door, her breathing ragged and her heart pounding as though it would burst through her ribs. She heard Paul call to her, then he was thumping on the door. Fearfully, she watched it shake, praying he would not be able to force it open.

'Go away!' she yelled. 'Get out!'

There was a low groan, then silence. Andie listened, but no further sounds came from the other side of the door. She strained her ears for the sound of a door closing, but heard nothing. The crickets outside were noisy and the air-conditioner seemed louder than usual. Had he gone? Or was he still lurking outside her door? She had no intention of looking. She lay on her bed, still listening, still shaking from her ordeal, and slowly the night passed. She must have dozed off, because she twice woke with a start, not knowing what had disturbed her.

Her alarm went off at the usual time. She must have

set it instinctively. She got up and crossed to the door, hesitating before she unbolted it. She opened the door slowly and heaved a sigh of relief. The passage was empty; the house was silent. Paul must have gone last night. Well, of course he had. She'd made it quite clear there was no point in his staying.

She walked along the passage and pushed open the door—then recoiled with shock. Paul was sitting at the kitchen table, a cup of black coffee in front of him. He heard her involuntary gasp and looked up. He was smiling, a contrite, please-forgive-me smile.

'Get out, Paul,' Andie said quietly. 'Now!' She watched him warily. He might have a hangover, but he wasn't drunk now as he had been last night. She was even more vulnerable now than then.

He lifted a hand defensively. 'It's all right, Andie. I was a bit under the weather last night—sorry. And seeing you again. . .'

'Get out, Paul,' she repeated, as she began shaking again.

'All right, all right, I'm going,' he said testily. 'You don't begrudge me a coffee, do you? That couch in the living-room isn't the most comfortable I've slept on.'

Andie felt on the verge of hysteria. His petulance was almost funny, but she dared not laugh. 'You should have gone back to the house.'

He looked sheepish. 'Couldn't make it, sweetheart. I just managed to crawl to the couch and I flaked out.' He laughed mockingly. 'You weren't in any danger, darling!'

Andie felt she would fragment if this went on much longer. 'Please go, Paul,' she begged. 'I have to go to work.'

He rose and came towards her. She shrank back, ready to run, but then instinctively realised he was not going to molest her. His libido wasn't in such good shape this morning. He put two fingers under her chin, then dropped a kiss on her mouth. 'Just for old times' sake,' he said. 'You're still a smasher, Andie. . .'

She pushed him away and he walked past her to the front door. He turned and gave her a little apologetic wave, saying, 'See you later!' as he departed, leaving the front door wide open.

'The nerve!' she exploded. She followed to close the door, and saw Paul slowly making his way up the side of the house, shoulders hunched, a figure of dejection. She could almost find it in her to feel sorry for him. Then she saw the Range Rover. Paul raised a hand in greeting, and Cam stopped. The two men spoke briefly, then the Range Rover drove off, wheels skidding, as Cam turned more abruptly than usual into the street.

Andie had no illusions as to what Cam must be thinking, even if Paul had not said what she assumed he would have done. She crashed the door shut and forced herself to get ready for work.

CHAPTER TEN

THE ambulance was in the bay in front of the Casualty entrance when Andie drove through the front gates and swung her car into her usual parking spot. The two paramedics who operated it were carrying in a stretcher.

Automatically, she secured her car—something she had never got out of the habit of doing, although nobody in Boobera ever seemed to—with more speed than usual, and half ran into the hospital. One thing she had become used to was expecting to be needed at the drop of a hat. Small country hospitals with minimum staff were not at all like big city complexes.

She almost cannoned into Reba. 'What's the emergency?' she asked.

'Oh, good, you're here,' said Reba with relief. 'I think we've got a prem—thirty-two weeks, according to the mother's calculations. I'm trying to get Barry, but he isn't answering his beeper—must be on the blink again. And Doc Warrington's away.'

'Where's Cam?' Andie asked at once. 'I saw him leave the house more than half an hour ago.'

Reba looked hard at her. 'Is that so? Funny, he hasn't arrived here.' Her face showed intense anxiety. 'Oh, why do they always vanish off the face of the earth when they're most needed? Look, will you see to her, Andie, while I get the incubator organised? I think she's going to deliver any minute.'

Andie flung on her uniform, clipped on her fob watch, and slid her feet into comfortable ward shoes. Within minutes she was in the delivery-room, where a very anxious Marion was trying to comfort the patient.

'Her name's Narelle,' she told Andie. 'She's from an outlying cattle station.'

'It's too soon,' the young woman was crying, 'much too soon. I'm going to lose it!'

Andie caught hold of her wrist and felt for the pulse. 'No, you're not. Just relax. Take a deep breath. . .and again. . .'

Narelle clutched Andie's hand. 'I—I wanted to have it the natural way.'

'Sure,' said Andie. 'But if things get too bad we'll help you with a painkiller. Just tell us when you want it.'

'Where's Dr Lester? I want Dr Lester!' the girl cried, half hysterically.

'Coming,' Andie assured her, although she wasn't sure that he was. 'Just take it easy, Narelle. . .it's going to be all right.'

'I'm going to lose it,' the girl whimpered, tears streaming down her face. 'I should have come for my check-ups, but we were busy, and I felt great right up until yesterday.'

'When was your last check-up?' Andie asked.

Narelle bit her lip. 'I only came in once after Dr Lester confirmed I was pregnant. I didn't think I needed to, I was so well.'

Andie stroked her hand. 'Where's your husband?'

'Away,' said the girl miserably. 'He went down to the sales in Adelaide the day before yesterday. He's not due back till the end of the week.' Her face contorted and she cried out as another contraction racked her.

Andie held her hand tightly and helped as much as she could. Thirty-two weeks was not too far off full-time, she was thinking optimistically. The baby had a good chance of survival, unless there was some under-lying reason for the premature birth.

'Is there anywhere we can contact your husband?' she asked.

The young mother nodded. 'I told Sister Luscombe.'

Reba hurried in to say, 'Cam's on the way. He just answered his beeper. And I've left a message for Dave, Narelle.'

'Unless Cam hurries, I think he's going to miss the main feature,' Andie said calmly, gently wiping perspiration from the patient's forehead.

Reba nodded. 'Do you like delivering babies?' she asked as another nurse helped them into sterile gowns and provided surgical gloves.

'Yes, but not premature ones,' answered Andie. 'They're so fragile. Is the incubator ready?'

Reba nodded. 'Trust Peg to get the flu. She'll be livid she missed this.'

Andie felt the usual nervous flutter inside her as she prepared to deliver the baby. She had delivered many babies since she had done her midwifery, but the nervousness and the sense of anticipation she had felt the very first time had never left her. The miracle of a new life bursting into an alien world always thrilled her and brought a lump to her throat.

Narelle's baby came quickly. He was small, wizened and blue. And without doubt he was dead.

Andie heard Reba's swift intake of breath, felt the shudder of disappointment that made the charge nurse's hands shake as she removed the baby from between the mother's legs. They looked at each other, stricken, while Narelle, exhausted, moaned softly, apparently unaware as yet that she had given birth. She was still desperately pushing.

She groaned loudly and began panting heavily. Andie looked from her face to her pelvis, startled. 'Keep up the oxygen,' she said quietly. 'I don't believe this, but. . .'

Reba placed the mask over the patient's nose and mouth, and her eyes registered amazement too as a second baby's head appeared. 'Twins!' she breathed, in a whisper too low for Narelle to hear. Once again

Andie gently swabbed the closed eyes and wiped the
tiny nose and mouth with gauze to remove the mucus.
She felt for the foetal cord, found to her relief that it
was exactly as it should be, and then with a final
convulsive jerk from Narelle the wrinkled red body
covered in the soft downy hair not unusual in prema-
tures slid smoothly into its new environment.

Narelle now knew instinctively that her ordeal was
over. 'Is it all right?' she gasped. 'What is it? A girl or
a boy?'

'A lovely little girl,' Reba told her, holding out
sterile towels to wrap her in, as Andie held the tiny
baby up and she gave her first cry.

'Well done! It seems I'm a shade too late.'

Andie turned to find Cam in the room. He was
wearing a gown and mask, and only his eyes were
visible. While Reba placed the baby in her mother's
arms, Andie took Cam to one side and explained what
had happened. 'She was sure she was going to lose the
baby,' she whispered. 'She didn't know she was expecting twins.' She added, 'I thought perhaps we wouldn't
tell her yet.'

Cam nodded agreement. 'Identical or fraternal?'

'A boy and a girl. The girl's larger and looks healthy,
but we've got the incubator ready.'

'I wonder why she didn't know she was expecting
twins?' Cam added drily. 'Barry must be slipping.'

'It seems she didn't bother about check-ups after the
first time. She felt well and didn't think it was necessary. It was a long way to come, after all. She couldn't
have had any tests either, I presume.'

Cam nodded. 'Why isn't Barry here?'

'I don't know. Reba couldn't raise him on his beeper
or the phone.'

'What, again?' His eyes were boring into hers, and
Andie burst out, 'Cam—what you saw this morning, it
wasn't. . .whatever Paul said. . .'

His lids lowered slightly and he said angrily, 'I don't

care what it was, Andie. The way you and Paul conduct your private life doesn't interest me in the slightest. And please, don't bring it to work! Now, perhaps we should transfer this baby to the incubator.'

Andie bit her lip, regretting the impulse that had made her speak. She could hardly have chosen a worse moment. She was still stinging from Cam's harsh words later when she took her coffee break. She was alone in the small nurses' room, and, if she hadn't been afraid Reba or Marion or one of the others might come in, she would have given way to tears.

She would not be able to stick it out for much longer, she thought. Not now. Seeing Cam every day would not be a consolation, as she'd hoped, it would simply wear her down, turn her into an emotional wreck. Even when he realised that she was not going back to Paul, it wouldn't make any difference. He would still think she had contemplated it. He would still think her a vacillating, silly woman, and Paul was never going to admit to Cam that he had been the one in the wrong. Not unless she agreed to marry him again, and that she would never do.

After the flurry of activity in the delivery-room that morning, things quietened down. Andie performed her routine duties automatically, but her mind was distant, her thoughts churning like a whirlpool even as she chatted cheerfully with her patients and attended to their needs.

For once the day seemed to drag. She longed for it to be over, but she did not want to go home. She was fearful that Paul might try to talk to her again. Her throat went dry every time she thought about another confrontation with her ex-husband. She didn't doubt that he would still try to persuade her. She had run away from his persistence once; she could do so again, she thought. She could just pack her bags and leave. She didn't want to leave Reba in the lurch, but what else could she do? It was going to be intolerable staying here.

The clock was still moving slowly towards the end of her shift, when the second emergency of the day occurred.

'I just hope they're not coming in threes!' exclaimed Reba.

'You don't mean another prem?' Andie asked, throwing up her hands.

'No, thank goodness.' Reba's face was grave. 'But it's serious. It's Madeleine Trentham. She went down with this instant flu yesterday, and now it looks as though she might have pneumonia.'

'Madeleine? Oh, no! Cam was over there on Saturday, and she was all right then. One of her staff had the flu, and he said the girl was all right, she just needed rest and lots of fluids.'

'Well, it seems Madeleine is more susceptible. She had a bout once before, about a year ago. She was hospitalised for a couple of weeks then.'

'What's happening this time?' asked Andie.

'Cam's going to get her, of course.'

'In the Cessna?'

'Yes. He wants you to go with him. I know you're off duty, but will you?'

Andie ran her tongue nervously over dry lips. She didn't want to go. Before she could reply, Cam burst in on them. 'Coming, Andie?' He had taken it for granted that she would.

Reba fled to answer a persistently ringing telephone, leaving them alone. Andie resisted his demand. 'Cam, I. . .' she began.

He looked at her steadily. 'I may need you. Besides, I want to talk to you.'

'Do we have anything to say? I thought you said——'

'I do now,' he said curtly. 'Come on, we'll have to

get a move on if we're to get Madeleine back before dark.'

Andie didn't argue. She felt she was being carried along on a tide of inevitability, and she was too weary to fight it.

Cam maintained almost complete silence until they had been in the air for ten minutes. Andie stared out of the plane window as the township receded behind them and disappeared into ground haze. The Ranges were stark and formidable in the harsh afternoon light, hot reds, browns and ochre contrasting with dense shadows and an enamelled cobalt sky.

Finally Cam spoke. 'Paul has told me the truth about the break-up of your marriage.'

Andie was shocked speechless. As the words still seemed to echo around the aeroplane cabin, she dredged up a whisper. 'He has?'

Cam was staring straight ahead through the windscreen, his profile rigid. 'It seems you were telling the truth after all. I apologise. And I'm sorry for what you went through. I make no excuses for Paul.'

Andie felt as though she were disintegrating. 'There's no need. . .'

'No, I realise that. I just hope it works out this time,' said Cam.

She felt as though she was suffocating. 'Cam, I'm not going back to Paul.'

'Yes, I know you're reluctant—Paul told me. And it's understandable. That's why I've sent him up to Marshall's Creek for a few days, to give you breathing space. I told him he could hardly expect you to welcome him back with open arms after the way he'd treated you, even if you are still in love with him.'

I'm not, Andie wanted to scream at him, I'm in love with you. But the words remained stuck somewhere deep within her.

Cam obviously believed that Paul had slept with her last night, and that reconciliation was now just a matter of time. He was trying to help. It was his way of compensating for not believing her. She stared helplessly at the mountains, which suddenly seemed full of menace and foreboding.

'I'd really rather not talk about it any more,' she said. She did not want to talk about anything. She just wanted to crawl into a hole in the ground and curl up and stay there. What she would do was leave Boobera as soon as possible.

'Paul's plans for going into real estate seem pretty sound,' Cam went on. 'Not like some of the harebrained notions he's had. I think this time he'll stick with it, especially as he has a partner who's willing to put in considerable equity. An experienced partner and a sensible wife may be the making of him. I think perhaps the time has come to approve of your marriage, Andie.'

Andie felt the blackness closing in on her, stifling her. Paul was using her again, using her to get Cam to recommend the release of his money, convinced she would do what he wanted. Convinced, like Cam, that she still loved him or could be persuaded that she did. She stole a glance at Cam. His face was tense. She knew how anxious he must be about Madeleine. He was talking to her about Paul, but his mind must be more on Madeleine.

Her continuing silence drew him to look at her. 'I'm sorry,' he said. 'I know you want time to think. I'm not trying to pressurise you, just hoping to make amends for five years ago. I've often wondered if my decision influenced what happened later.'

Andie's control was shaky. She shouted at him angrily, 'Can't you just leave it, Cam? You told *me* not to bring my personal life to work. We're still at work, remember?' She ended on a gasping sob. 'Sorry. . .'

Cam flinched. She was right, of course. He shouldn't have brought the subject up, not when she was obviously going through a difficult time. He was only trying to redeem himself, and that wasn't fair.

Andie shrank as far away from him as her seatbelt would permit. This would soon be over. She just had to keep her mind concentrated on what they'd come for—to transport a patient to hospital—and do what was required of her. The fact that the patient would almost certainly marry Cam was irrelevant. The fact that she was in love with Cam herself was also irrelevant.

'Nearly there,' said Cam, breaking into her thoughts.

Andie saw the scattered buildings that must be Tourmaline coming up ahead. They buzzed the station homestead and she saw someone on the ground waving. Then Cam was banking the aircraft steeply and turning in a wide circle. Almost before she was aware of the airstrip, they were skimming the trees and moments later touched down with a few bumps.

'Not as well graded as ours,' Cam commented. 'Sorry for the bumpy ride.'

Andie wished he would stop being sorry for everything.

There was a vehicle waiting, driven by one of Madeleine's staff, a very worried young woman who introduced herself as Jenny.

'Thank heaven you've come,' she said, her face flooding with relief. 'I didn't know what to do. We thought she just had flu like a couple of the others have had recently, but last night she seemed worse. She wouldn't let us call the doctor then because she was expecting Mr Branson today—he's the man who's going to buy the property—but I phoned him this morning and told him she was ill and he'd better postpone his trip. She'll be mad as hell at me, but what else could I do?'

'I'm sure you did the right thing,' Cam assured her.

The airstrip was not so far away as at Marshall's

Creek, and in hardly more than five minutes they were
walking into the homestead. Madeleine was clearly
very ill. Her breathing was stertorous and her temperature dangerously high. She was on the verge of delir-
ium. Cam's deepening anxiety showed in his face as he
clasped her hand.

'I'll give her a shot of penicillin,' he said to Andie.
'We must get her to hospital as fast as we can.'

As they were about to lift her on to the stretcher,
Madeleine opened her eyes and for a few moments
was lucid. 'Cam. . .' she breathed. 'Oh, darling, it's so
good to see you. I'm afraid I've got the flu.'

He squeezed her hand. 'You'll be all right soon.
We're taking you to hospital.'

'No, I can't—Phil Branson's coming today. I've only
got flu.' She made a futile effort to sit up.

'You've got pneumonia,' said Cam, pushing her
back on the pillows. 'You need hospital treatment.
Jenny has advised Mr Branson, and he's coming up
later in the week.'

Madeleine was too weak to protest any further. She
closed her eyes and gave herself up to their
ministrations.

The next morning, Andie told Reba she wanted to
resign. Just the look on Reba's face was almost enough
to make her change her mind.

'You can't,' said Reba emphatically. 'Andie, no, you
can't! You're the best nurse we've had here in years.
We can't do without you.' She went on almost angrily,
'I thought you liked it here.'

Andie felt close to tears. 'I do, but. . . Reba, there
are personal reasons why I must go. I'm not sure I can
tell you about them without breaking down. . .so
please don't ask me to.'

Reba slid a comforting arm around her shoulders.
'Is it anything to do with Barry?'

'No, of course not. There's never been anything between Barry and me.'

'Well, it must be Cam.'

'No,' Andie lied. 'It's. . .well, it's my ex-husband. He's found out where I am, and he—he's harassing me.'

Reba was shocked. 'You're not. . . He's not a wife-basher?'

'No, no, nothing like that. Reba, I'm in a bit of an emotional muddle. I need to think a few things out, and I can't do that here.'

Reba clamped her lips together, disappointment clouding her eyes. 'I'm sorry, Andie, I won't pry any more. When do you want to go?'

'As soon as possible.'

'You'll have to tell Matron. You're supposed to give a month's notice, but Peg's pretty sympathetic. She won't hold you to it.' Reba drew in a deep breath and let it out slowly. 'Can you stay till the end of the week? That'll give me time to rearrange rosters and see about a replacement. We probably won't get anyone that quickly, but. . .' She broke off on another deep sigh of resignation.

'I'm sorry,' Andie said, 'I feel so guilty. I hate to let you down like this.'

Reba slid a comforting arm around her shoulders. 'Look, Andie, I know you wouldn't be doing this if you didn't have a very good reason. You have to do what you have to do in this life, and I just hope things work out for you.' She gave a stoical grin. 'We'll manage!'

'Perhaps I'd better go and see Peg now,' Andie suggested, 'and get it over with.'

By Thursday everyone knew Andie was leaving. There was some consternation amongst the other nurses, but probably because Reba had advised them not to, nobody pressed her to explain her reasons. Barry

broached the subject when she was sterilising and
putting away instruments from the examination trolley
after he had visited a couple of his patients. As they
had visited the wards together, she had sensed that he
knew, but he had said nothing until afterwards.

'What's the problem?' he asked directly.

'Personal.' She tried to convey firmly with her eyes
that she would not answer further questions.

Barry gave a rueful smile. 'Let me guess. You've
fallen in love with Cam.'

Andie feared her sharp intake of breath gave her
away. 'No,' she denied. 'What on earth makes you
think that?' She covered her dismay with surprise and
hoped she was convincing.

He assumed a soulful expression. 'Well, it certainly
isn't because of me.'

'I'm glad you don't flatter yourself.'

Barry laughed, and, as she removed her gloves,
grasped her hand. 'You know, Andie, if I were the
settling-down type, you're just the sort of woman I'd
choose to settle down with.'

'Thanks for the compliment, but Reba's more your
type, only you don't seem to have noticed.'

He didn't laugh again as she expected. He said
soberly, 'I've noticed, Andie, but what hope have I
got? She's married to the job—and Boobera. I'm not
sure I can stay here all my life, and she wouldn't
budge, even if she did fancy me.'

'She fancies you,' Andie told him, glad to have
shifted the focus of their conversation. 'Or rather she
suffers you. You ought to take Reba a bit more
seriously, Barry. Can't you see she's being defensive
because she thinks you're just an incurable flirt? She's
erected a barrier between you because she has to
pretend not to be hurt. Reba's a very vulnerable and
very caring person. You ought to try and get to know
her properly. You might even begin to feel like settling
down!'

Barry looked a bit sheepish. 'You sound like the lady in the women's magazine agony column!'

'I don't think it would take much to make Reba fall in love with you,' Andie dared to say. 'And people in love can usually work out compromises on all their other problems.' If she could just give Barry the push he needed, she thought, it would help to salve her conscience over leaving poor Reba in the lurch.

Barry asked doubtfully, 'Was she jealous when I took you out?'

'She pretended not to be, but I'm sure she was.'

'Would you believe it?' he exclaimed. 'I didn't think she cared two pins for me. She's always a bit brusque, quick to criticise—like last Monday when I didn't answer my beeper, she read me the riot act, even though it wasn't my fault, the damned thing was faulty.'

'She hides her personal feelings well,' Andie said. 'It isn't always easy to do.'

He eyed her narrowly. 'You're not hiding yours as well as you think, Andie. I saw it coming right from the first. It's a pity you had to fall for Cam. Nice guy, but I guess Madeleine got there first.'

Andie shoved soiled towels in the laundry bin. 'You don't know what you're talking about.'

'OK, I'll say no more. I wish I could do the same for you as you've done for me.'

'Good luck!' Andie said. She wished he could too. Other people's problems always seemed to be more easily solved than one's own.

'Goodbye, Andie, in case I don't see you again,' Barry said. 'I hope things work out for you.' He raised her hand to his lips. 'Nice knowing you.'

He turned to go, and as he went out, Cam came in. Andie tried to find something to keep her hands busy, but there was little left to do.

'You're leaving,' Cam said, folding his arms across

his chest and standing closer than was comfortable for her.

'Yes. On Friday.'

'What about Paul?'

Andie took a step back and stared out of the window. 'What about him?'

His voice bored into the back of her head. 'He wants you back. Are you sure running away is the best way to act, Andie? Why don't you come up to Marshall's Creek this weekend and talk it over with him? I'm sure you can work something out.'

'You're so keen for me to marry him now!' She turned angrily. 'Why?'

'I've realised that you're not the person I once thought you were. You're the kind of woman Paul needs. I know now you didn't walk out on him, so if you still love him, give him another chance.'

She looked into the anxious dark eyes pleading with her and to her horror found herself wavering. It was ironical. Cam wanted her to remarry his brother because he now saw her as the bulwark Paul needed, and because he felt some responsibility for the failure of their marriage. Suddenly she was weakening, not for Paul's sake, but for Cam's. Supposing she and Paul did remarry, perhaps it would work if she tried harder, and if he was different. She would never love him as she loved Cam, but then she never had. And if she couldn't spend the rest of her life with Cam, then perhaps it might as well be with Paul.

She was appalled at the drift of her thoughts. But her love for Cam, she realised, could drive her to do anything he wanted, and he wanted her to go back to Paul. She gave a grim little smile. Once he had pleaded with her not to marry Paul, now he was pleading with her to do so.

But her decision was not final. She needed time to think, to adjust. 'I'll be driving back to Melbourne on

Saturday morning,' she told him. 'I'll see Paul there. Not too soon. Tell him, in a week or so.'

He accepted this as her final word, and the relief that softened the rigidity of his facial muscles almost made her feel gratified. She did not notice the pain he was endeavouring to conceal.

'I'll tell him,' he said.

Andie had managed to keep away from Madeleine's room. She knew Cam was in and out a lot, that he had been attentive almost twenty-four hours a day during the first few days of her illness. But on Friday morning she was obliged to take an out-of-hours visitor in to see her. It was Mr Branson, the man who was to purchase Tourmaline.

Madeleine was propped in bed in a lacy bedjacket, her auburn hair swept up in an attractive tumble of curls on top of her head, her face lightly made up. She looked pale still, but the slight gauntness in her face made her look almost waif-like and very appealing.

'Phil!' She held out her hands. 'At last!'

'They wouldn't let me see you before.' He clasped her hands and bent to kiss her. 'Not family yet! How are you, my dear? You had me really worried for a few days.'

Madeleine said, 'Andie, do you think you could get Phil a cup of coffee?'

Andie sent Lenore back with the coffee and biscuits. She was puzzled by Mr Branson's remark about 'not family yet', and decided she must have misheard. She glanced at the clock for the umpteenth time that morning. Only a few more hours to go, then say goodbye to everyone, go home and say goodbye to Jean, go early to bed, and set off at dawn on the long drive back. She'd spend a couple of days in Adelaide, she decided, and by the time she reached Melbourne perhaps she would have accustomed herself to the idea of going back to Paul.

It was just after lunch when Madeleine pressed her call button. Andie was not within range and someone else went to see what she wanted.

'She wants to see you, Andie,' Vicky said.

'Oh, why me?'

Vicky shrugged. 'She didn't say. To say goodbye, I suppose.'

Andie steeled herself and walked reluctantly down the corridor to Madeleine Trentham's room. It wasn't that she didn't like her, it was just that Madeleine reminded her too much of her futile longings for Cam, and she couldn't cope with the waves of jealousy that washed over her and made her feel guilty.

'Hello, Andie.' Madeleine was reading a magazine.

'You're looking a lot better,' Andie told her truthfully. 'I expect you'll be able to go home in a couple more days.'

Madeleine motioned her to take the chair near the bed. 'I hope so.' She studied Andie's face for a moment. 'I hear you're leaving?'

'Yes, I'm afraid so.'

Madeleine smiled. 'It's because of Cam, I suppose.'

'I don't know what you're. . .' Andie was mortified. For Madeleine to have guessed. She was bound to tell Cam, and that would ruin everything.

Madeleine leaned confidingly towards her. 'Andie, I didn't realise that was why you were avoiding me, why I saw every other nurse in this place several times a day but never you. It was only when I told Reba a little while ago that I was engaged—I was so happy I had to tell someone right away—that the penny dropped. She was so much more delighted than I'd expected a mere acquaintance to be! She admitted that she'd thought, that quite a lot of people had thought, Cam and I would be getting married.'

Andie was speechless. She managed only to say, 'But you said you're engaged.'

'Yes, I am.' Madeleine waved her left hand to show

off the diamond that glittered there. 'Dear, darling
Phil Branson. He was a great friend of Hugo's. He's
going to buy Tourmaline, as an investment. He said
that when he was told how ill I was, he was frantic,
and decided he had to marry me and look after me
properly. Now isn't that romantic! And the thing is,
I've now realised I'm much fonder of dear Phil than
I'd imagined.'

There was a pounding in Andie's ears that could
only stem from a racing heartbeat. 'But you gave me
the impression right from the start that you and Cam
were. . .'

'Lovers?' Madeleine chuckled. 'I'm sure Cam's no
angel, but we weren't lovers, Andie, I swear it. I'm
very fond of Cam, and for a while, when he helped me
over a bad patch when Hugo died, I imagined I was in
love with him, but I soon realised he wasn't in love
with me. I was a bit jealous, though, when I saw very
obvious signs that he was about to fall in love with
someone else—you.'

'Me?'

'Of course! I thought you'd have discovered each
other by now. I'm willing to bet every penny I own the
poor man's probably distraught because you're leaving.
He probably thinks there's someone else. There isn't,
is there?'

Andie slowly shook her head.

'Well, then, before you go and ruin both your lives,
I suggest you go and find Cam and lay your cards on
the table. If you ask me, you've got a royal flush!'

It took Andie some moments after she had left
Madeleine to convince herself that what she had heard
might be true. Dared she confront Cam, betray herself? What if Madeleine was wrong? She would be
humiliated. Cam had been so anxious for her to marry
Paul again. Surely if he was in love with her. . . I can't
marry Paul, she thought suddenly. Not even to please
Cam. I can't. Whatever made me imagine I could?

She went along to Cam's office, but he was not
there. She saw Reba coming along the corridor. The
charge nurse was grinning from ear to ear. 'Looking
for Cam?'

'Ye-es.'

'He's around somewhere. I saw him a few minutes
ago.' She hugged Andie. 'Good luck!'

Andie saw Vicky coming out of the operating suite.
'Is Cam there?' she asked.

Vicky shook her head. 'He left a few minutes ago.'

'Left? Went home, you mean?'

'I think so.' Vicky crossed to a window overlooking
the car park. 'The Range Rover's gone.'

Andie had never felt so deflated in her life. When
Reba discovered what had happened she insisted that
Andie go too.

'Now!' ordered Reba. She smiled happily. 'No need
to say goodbye. You'll be back on Monday, I hope.
Cam'll let you give a bit more notice, I expect!'

Andie tried to play it down. 'Reba, you're jumping
to conclusions, and so is Madeleine. You don't know
. . .the full story. . .it's much more complicated than
you imagine.'

'Well, the sooner you sort it out the better,' Reba
declared. 'Go on, off you go. And I want to see you
here Monday!'

Andie drove back to the annexe at Cam's house,
trembling with apprehension. When she turned in at
the gate and saw the driveway empty, her heart sank.
Cam was not there. She knocked on the door. Jean
opened it and looked as disapproving as she had ever
since Andie had told her she was leaving.

'Has Cam been home?' Andie asked.

'Yes. He left again a few minutes ago.'

'Damn!' Andie dragged a hand wearily across her
forehead. 'He's gone to Marshall's Creek?'

Jean confirmed it, and suddenly Andie could stand
no more. The iron control she had been keeping on

herself all week broke and she fell on the housekeeper's neck and wept.

'I think you'd better come in and have a cup of tea
and tell me all about it,' Jean said, holding the weeping
girl in her arms and gently drawing her into the house.

CHAPTER ELEVEN

ANDIE had meant to leave at dawn, but she was so emotionally drained after confessing everything to Jean the night before that she overslept. Jean, who had insisted on putting her to bed in the house, had not wakened her, deeming it best to let the girl recover her strength before the new ordeal she still had to face.

So it was after an early lunch, provided by Jean, that Andie finally set off for Marshall's Creek. She had taken Jean's advice and intended to have it out with both Paul and Cam. Jean was not willing to say whether she thought Cam was in love with her, but she made it quite clear she thought he was a fool not to be.

'He didn't tell me you'd been married to Paul,' she said. 'I'd never met his brother before, and I have to say I wouldn't have picked Paul for a husband for you. We all make mistakes, love, and I believe you'd be making the same mistake if you married him again. You can't be happy with one man if you love another. It's better to stay single.' She had looked wistful for a moment, as though it was something she knew about.

Andie found the road rugged but not too taxing on her driving ability at first. As she drove further and further into the mountains and finally started the long climb up to the plateau, the road narrowed down to a wheel-rutted track and the going was heavier. There were dark clouds banking up ominously over the distant Ranges and the air was oppressive. There were streaks of lightning across a distant cloud bank, and she heard a faint rumble of thunder.

Nargun dashed to meet her as she pulled up outside

the homestead, and as she stooped to fondle his head Moira appeared on the veranda.

'Andie!' she exclaimed. 'What are you doing here?'

Andie ran across to her. 'I have to see Cam and Paul. . .'

Moira looked perplexed and anxious. 'Paul's gone,' she said.

'Gone? When?'

'This morning.' Moira pursed her lips. 'There was a big row, Andie, between him and Cam. I don't know what about.'

Andie was distraught. 'So where's Cam?'

'He said he was going for a swim.'

'The waterhole?'

'It's the only place. Andie. . .'

'I'll take one of the trail-bikes,' Andie decided.

Moira glanced at the sky. 'Can't you wait until he comes back?'

Andie was in a fever of impatience. She wanted to see Cam now, on his own.

Moira saw it was useless to argue. 'Take care,' she said.

Andie raced to the shed and wheeled out one of the trail-bikes, mounted it and headed off along the track to the waterhole. She had ridden about halfway before she realised that the distant storm clouds were moving across the Ranges towards Marshall's Creek. There was a sudden drop in temperature, and the great jagged walls of red rock surrounding her were turning a deep and ominous purple.

Low cloud began to swirl above her like smoke. The lightning flashes were closer and followed quickly by deep rolls of thunder. As large drops of rain began to spatter on the dry earth, Andie realised she had been foolish to ride out when a storm was imminent. Cam wouldn't think much of her common sense.

She would have turned back, but she was a long way from the homestead, with no shelter behind her, and from previous rides she was sure she must be close to a large overhang she remembered seeing. She urged her bike on, hoping it was not too far away. It was growing darker now even though it was not yet dusk. One vivid flash of lightning split the sky, nearly blinding her, and the thunderclap almost unseated her, it was so explosive.

With the rain now beating into her face, it took all Andie's strength not to fall off the bike, but ahead of her she saw the rocky outcrop that would provide shelter. As she came to within a hundred metres of it, she saw Cam. He was going to get there before she did.

For a moment he was out of sight as he came to a dip in the track, then he breasted the rise that brought him to within a few metres of the overhang. Another flash of lightning was so close that Andie gave an involuntary scream. The storm was all around her and lightning forked right into the ground on the track just in front of her, almost blinding her. She braked as the clap of thunder that followed the lightning deafened her.

Then there was silence, except for the hissing of the rain sheeting down, while the storm recharged for another display of pyrotechnics. Andie peered through the rain, but could not see Cam now. She wondered if he had seen her.

The bike's engine was wet and it was coughing and spluttering. It was almost impossible to push it through the mud. For moments she thought she would have to abandon it and run the rest of the way. Desperately she urged the machine over a rise and down the slope to the overhang, expecting to see Cam sheltering there. What she did see brought a horrified gasp to her lips.

'Cam!' His bike was on its side, one wheel still spinning, and he was spreadeagled beside it, not far from the overhang. He was lying ominously still.

The engine in Andie's bike finally gave out. She

flung it aside and ran to him. He couldn't be dead, he mustn't be. She loved him and she needed to tell him. It was too cruel. She flung herself down beside him.

'Cam. . . Cam. . .oh, God, please don't let him be dead. Cam, I love you, I love you. I love you so much. . .'

A desperate sobbing racked her, but she forced herself to think rationally. He *might* not be dead.

'Resuscitate,' she told herself urgently. 'Just in case. Always try.'

She wasn't strong enough to drag him through the mud to the overhang. She would have to do it here in the open, in the pouring rain. But that was impossible. She removed his helmet and tipped his head back, placing one hand under his chin. She took a deep breath and was about to place her mouth over his when a long shuddering groan escaped his lips, making her jerk back. Startled, then overjoyed, she whispered, 'Thank you, thank you, thank you! Oh, Cam, I love you so much, I couldn't bear it if you died.' She laid her cheek against his for a moment, then quickly straightened up.

He groaned and his eyelids flickered. The rain was running off his face and he lifted a hand to try and wipe it. 'Andie! What the hell are you doing here? What happened?'

'You crashed—I think you must have been struck by lightning. Are you hurt?' she asked frantically. 'Can you move into the shelter of the overhang? It isn't far, but I can't move you on my own. If you can help a bit. . .'

Slowly he sat up. 'I'm OK—I think.' He dragged a muddy hand across his brow. 'Just—wet!'

They scrambled into the shelter of the rocky overhang. There was dry sand there and the rain was driving across the overhang, not into it. Cam was still a bit dazed. He looked at Andie in amazement. 'How come. . .?' Then a slow realisation brought a wonder-

ing expression into his eyes. 'Andie. . .a moment ago
out there, did I hear you say. . .? Was I hallucinating,
or did you actually say. . .?'

Andie's teeth were chattering and she could not
speak. She had endured too many shocks.

Cam pulled her into his arms and held her close.
'You're cold?'

She managed to whisper, 'No, just shocked, I think.
I thought you were dead.'

He removed her helmet and smoothed her pale hair
back from her face. Her eyes were misty with tears.
'Andie, was it just wishful thinking on my part, or did
you. . .did you say you loved me?'

Tears were streaming down her face now, mingling
with the wetness of the rain. She nodded mutely.

'But you said. . . I felt sure you'd go back to Paul—
that in the end you'd find you still loved him.'

'No. I stopped loving him a long time ago,' Andie
told him.

'Then why. . .?' The dark eyes she loved so dearly
were perplexed.

She looked at him helplessly, tears streaming down
her cheeks, unable to speak.

Cam insisted, 'But it was Paul who deserted you.'

She just continued to look at him, marvelling that
he was not dead after all, swamped by an emotion so
powerful that she hardly knew how to handle it.

He pulled her head against him, holding her cheek
against his heart, and she felt its reassuring beat with
overwhelming joy. They sat huddled in each other's
arms for some time.

Finally Cam said slowly, 'Why are you here?'

Andie could still manage only the briefest of expla-
nations. 'I—I thought you were going to marry
Madeleine. I thought it would make you happy if I
went back to Paul, but I didn't really want to. For a
while I just didn't care what I did. Then I found out

that Madeleine was engaged to the man who's going to buy her property. . .'

'Phil Branson,' he interrupted. 'I thought she might. I'm glad about that.' He kissed her mouth softly. 'Go on. . .'

Andie blushed. 'She said. . . Oh, Cam I hardly dared to believe it might be true, even when Jean said. . . It was agony missing you yesterday. I had to know, even if I made a fool of myself. I was going to have it out with Paul and you, get everything out in the open honestly. I knew I couldn't marry Paul again, not even to please you. You were right—we should never have married in the first place.'

'I didn't want you to marry in the second place either,' Cam said softly. 'I was trying to be fair, trying not to think of myself, because I thought you still loved him. When he told me he'd left you, not the other way round as he'd pretended to try and gain my sympathy, I was sure you'd forgive him in the end.'

Andie shook her head vehemently. 'Moira said you had a row and he left.'

His face darkened with pain. 'Yes. I'd told him that if he and you married again I'd recommend the release of half the money now, the rest when the business was off the ground, but not before twelve months. He wouldn't have that. He ranted and raved, and I knew that my fears that he was using you again, that he didn't really love you, were true. So I told him he could have the whole of his inheritance providing he never saw you again.'

'Cam!' she exclaimed.

He looked at her with agony in his eyes. 'It was a terrible thing to do, but I couldn't bear the thought of you being made unhappy again, loving him and being punished for it. He's a weak, selfish man, Andie, and because he's my brother I keep trying to pretend otherwise. I thought that if he loved you he would never accept such a condition.'

Andie said sadly, 'But he did.'

'Yes.' He took a deep breath. 'Oh, he made a fuss, shed a few crocodile tears that didn't fool me this time, and finally left. His parting words were, "Well, now I've got what I wanted, you can have what you want." I knew he meant you, but I didn't believe it was possible. I was so shaken up by it all I rode out to the waterhole to be alone to think. I'd meddled in your life once again, and I still wasn't sure I'd had a right to.'

'I'm so glad you did,' Andie murmured, snuggling close. She lifted her face to his, smiling hesitantly. 'What do you want, Cam?'

He touched his lips to hers. 'You, Andie. I always did. From the moment I saw you in London, wild and wilful and so desirable, it was painful to look at you, because I wanted you. But you wanted my brother. My responsibility towards him clashed with my own emotions, and you suffered as a result. When you arrived in Boobera I was shattered. Seeing you revived my feelings and working with you intensified them. But you weren't interested in me. I was the ogre who'd insulted you and might have wrecked your marriage. I tried to tell myself that you were just a flirt, as you had been all along. Just a girl with an untamed heart. You flirted with Barry, with Fritz, and I couldn't even be sure how you still felt about Paul. I kept firmly to the belief that you'd left Paul, even though in my heart of hearts I was doubting it. I was trying desperately not to fall in love with you, Andie. . .to stop wishing I could be the one to tame that fickle heart of yours.'

'And I was trying not to love you,' she whispered. 'I never had an affair with Barry, I didn't flirt with Fritz, although he did a bit with me, and that night Paul arrived he was drunk and I had to lock myself in my bedroom. He collapsed on the couch and slept there. In the morning I threw him out.'

Silently they looked at the rain, huddled together,

arms around each other. 'We're in a bit of a fix here,'
Cam said at last, his tone lighter. He smiled down at
Andie. 'I expect both the bikes have had it and we'd
never get through the mud anyway. We'll just have to
wait until we're rescued.'

'Rescued? How?' she asked.

'Everyone knows where we went. As soon as the
rain stops Fritz will come looking for us in the Toyota.
Bet you! This won't last much longer. We often get
storms and flash floods like this. Look, it's beginning
to ease off already, and the sky's lightening. The
thunder's way in the distance now. Fritz'll be here
soon.'

He brushed his lips against hers, and a shiver of pure
bliss made her tremble in his arms. 'We'd better make
the most of it,' he said softly. 'Don't you agree?'

'Oh, I definitely do,' breathed Andie.

4 MEDICAL ROMANCES
AND 2 FREE GIFTS
From Mills & Boon

Capture all the excitement, intrigue and emotion of the busy medical world by accepting four FREE Medical Romances, plus a FREE cuddly teddy and special mystery gift. Then if you choose, go on to enjoy 4 more exciting Medical Romances every month! Send the coupon below at once to:

MILLS & BOON READER SERVICE, FREEPOST
PO BOX 236, CROYDON, SURREY CR9 9EL.

NO STAMP REQUIRED

- - - ✂ - ✂ - - -

YES! Please rush me my 4 Free Medical Romances and 2 Free Gifts! Please also reserve me a Reader Service Subscription. If I decide to subscribe, I can look forward to receiving 4 Medical Romances every month for just £6.40, delivered direct to my door. Post and packing is free, and there's a free Mills & Boon Newsletter. If I choose not to subscribe I shall write to you within 10 days - I can keep the books and gifts whatever I decide. I can cancel or suspend my subscription at any time. I am over 18.

EP19D

Name (Mr/Mrs/Ms) _____

Address _____

_____

_____ Postcode _____

Signature _____

MEDICAL ROMANCE

The books for enjoyment this month are:

THE CALL OF LOVE Jenny Ashe
A HEART UNTAMED Judith Worthy
WAITING GAME Laura MacDonald
THE WESSEX SUMMER Sarah Franklin

♥ ♥ ♥ ♥ ♥

Treats in store!

Watch next month for the following absorbing stories:

SURGEON OF THE HEART Sharon Wirdnam
A GENTLE GIANT Caroline Anderson
DREAM OF NAPLES Lisa Cooper
HAND IN HAND Margaret Barker